Exercises of the Heart

Exercises of the Heart

Jan Greenberg

Farrar Straus Giroux / New York

For my mother, Lillian Schonwald,
lovingly remembered

Not out of curiosity, not just to exercise the heart . . .
But because being here means so much, and because all
that's here, vanishing so quickly, seems to need us
and strangely concerns us.

RILKE, *Duino Elegies: Ninth Elegy*

Exercises of the Heart

1

In my opinion, Friday after 3 P.M. wins the best-part-of-the-week award. All over America, bells ring and millions of kids start celebrating. School's out for the weekend . . . two whole days! Imagine us, from coast to coast, East, West, North, and South, standing, sitting, or lying in every conceivable position, breathing a huge simultaneous sigh of relief. What a mind-boggling thought!

Right at this auspicious moment, I'm curled into my favorite easy chair, the one my father loved, reading *To Kill a Mockingbird*. It tells the story of a girl named Scout who lives with her father, Atticus Finch, and her brother, Jem, in a sleepy Southern town. I can relate, since I live with my mother and little sister, Merlie, in Ladue, Missouri, the Midwest's sleepiest suburb. But there's one paragraph I can't seem to get past. Here Scout describes how she crawls into Atticus's lap every night while he reads aloud from the newspaper. I start thinking about my own father and all the times, after dinner, when I used to do the same thing. Like Scout, I learned to read by listening to the *Post Dispatch* and watching Dad point to the words. How I wish I was snuggled on his lap again, back in our old house on Buckingham Drive, as if nothing had ever changed. Keep reading, I tell myself, before you fall into a deep funk. Then the phone rings and saves me from making the effort.

"Are you alone, Roxie?" comes the voice of my best friend, Glo Stern. I can picture her talking into the phone, sprawled sideways on the floor, propped up on one elbow. Knowing Glo, she'll pester me until I stop what I'm doing (which is basically brooding) and make plans with her.

"I'm trying to read, but my mind keeps wandering."

"Of course it does. You don't really want to sit around your house on a Friday night *alone,* do you?" This time she says *alone* with all the disdain she can muster, as if being alone is the most pathetic state anyone could possibly find herself in. "Give your brain a rest and come over. Besides, Mother's locked in her studio, everyone else is busy, and I'm soooo bored." Glo hates to be by herself even for a minute. Between her sister, her parents, a house full of servants, and friends dropping in and out, Glo's accustomed to an adoring crowd. All that activity makes me batty, but still I'm drawn there like a magnet.

"Maybe I will. I seem to be stuck in the second chapter."

"Are you in one of your moods again?"

"It's just this book." And this chair and this room— which was once my father's study.

"You'd better get over here before you turn into a basket case." Glo's request sounds like a command. But maybe she's right.

"I'll go tell Mother. I don't think she's made other plans for us tonight." I know she has no plans. She never does, except to be with my Aunt Dorothy. But sometimes she gets irritated because I spend so much time at the Sterns'.

Downstairs, I find Mother perched on a ladder, applying white paint to the ceiling in the entrance hall. When we moved into this house, she and my father decided to repaint it themselves. They talked about how much fun it would be to do a project together to save money. But, for a lot of reasons, their "project" was never finished. As I look around at the cracks in the ceiling, the striped wallpaper peeling off the dining-room walls, the bay windows without drapes, I realize our house still has a half-finished look, as if we moved in but weren't quite sure we were going to stay.

It's been three years since my father died. Her working on the house again is a good sign. "This is terrific," I tell her. "I'm glad you're finally going to finish what you and ..." It makes me too sad to say "Dad" out loud. Mother's wearing her paint-spattered jeans and a white paper cap. Wisps of gray hair fall into her face.

"Roxie, you can help," she says in her halting voice. She points to a bucket of paint.

"Glo wants me to come over and spend the night."

"Oh, Roxie." She shakes her head. "You don't need to go *there*."

I stiffen—a funny tightness in my stomach. It's not that she won't let me go to Glo's house; she'll just act disapproving, pursing her lips or sighing. Sometimes I argue, but today I don't want to fight. I feel badly about leaving her all by herself.

"If I help you paint this room, may I go later?" She nods and goes back to her work, dipping the roller in the long container and sliding it carefully back and forth across the ceiling. It takes all her concentration. Mother doesn't have the coordination in her hand that she once had. For a while, we work in silence. We used to talk about things when I was younger, but in the last few years we haven't had much to say.

I'm so busy slapping paint on the wall, trying to get it over with, that I don't notice her climb down from the ladder to observe my progress. Suddenly she grabs the roller out of my hand and rams it to the floor. "This is a mess," she spits out. "Stop." There seems to be more paint over my clothes than there is on the wall. In several spots, uneven glops of paint drip down, like shiny white worms edging their way to the floor.

"It's not that bad. I can fix it easily," I say crossly, thinking that nothing I do pleases her anyway. "Here I stay home to help and all you do is complain."

"I can't stand this," she sputters. Mother has trouble talking, especially when she feels frustrated.

"So get Merlie to do it when she comes home. I'm leaving." Then I turn my back on her and stomp out. Mother never lets me get away with anything. I guess we have a communication problem. That's what she might call it in her social-worker lingo. But it goes beyond the generation gap for reasons that have nothing to do with typical mother–daughter stuff, back to a night five years ago when we still lived in our old house. It's a night I'll never forget. Our family had no control over what happened, and afterwards nothing else could ever be the same. There were no hints, no signs of an impending disaster. Everything just fell apart, as if we had an earthquake.

My father used to travel on business when he was head salesman for his company. While he was out of town, I would sleep with my mother in their big double bed, curled under their rose-colored satin comforter, with the hum of the humidifier lulling me into a deep sleep. The room smelled of Vitabath and my father's Aramis cologne.

I remember being in the middle of a wonderful dream when Mother woke me. "Get Dorothy," she said hoarsely. The room was pitch black except for the digital clock glowing. Three A.M.

"Leave me alone," I said, turning over. Then she shoved me. "Hey, stop it," I grumbled. At that point, Merlie, awakened by our voices, burst in and switched on the lights. Then I saw the bed. Thick, red vomit covered the sheets. My mother, half dazed, sat up, pressing her thumbs to her temple as if to keep her brains from spilling out.

"Get Dorothy," she said again in a cracked voice. Merlie screamed and went tearing off. I leaped out of bed, but I couldn't move. I was helpless. I remember feeling revulsion and, later, guilt, because it was my little sister who ran next door in the dark to Aunt Dorothy's place. Barefoot and in her nightgown, my aunt rushed in, with Merlie clutching her hand. By this time, Mother lay unconscious on the bed and I was scrunched in a corner, my face to the wall.

"Something's wrong with Mother," Merlie said, sobbing.

"Oh, my God, Franny," Aunt Dorothy cried, and grabbed the phone to call an ambulance.

I remember the sirens, the men carrying Mother out in a stretcher, and the handful of neighbors who gathered on the front lawn, offering to help when their help was no longer necessary.

Mother stayed in the hospital for a long time. I went to visit her only once. She was propped in a chair, wearing a blue robe with lace at the throat. The first thing I noticed was a jagged scar on her neck.

I had picked out new school clothes all by myself and wanted her to see them, to approve my choices. "Do you like this?" I asked, holding up a red plaid kilt. She smiled and nodded but didn't say anything. There were tears running down her cheeks, but she made no sound. "See, we're doing fine," I assured her. "Don't worry." I bent to kiss her cheek. Her skin felt burning hot, and she sat very still, as if she couldn't move. "She can't talk yet," my father told me when we were in the elevator going down.

The day she came home from the hospital, Merlie and I waited for her on the front porch. My father helped her out of the car. During those months in the hospital, her hair had turned gray. "Is that Mom?" Merlie asked, tugging on my hand. "She's so old."

Mother paused at the steps for a moment and looked at us. I waited for her to say something, but she just stood there.

"Don't cry, Franny," my father said. He turned to us. "She's crying because she can't say hello."

What does he mean, I thought. Why can't she say hello?

Later, Dad explained to Merlie and me what had happened to her. A bubble had formed on an artery in her neck. Pressure built until the bubble burst and flooded her brain with blood. "Aneurysm is the medical term," he said. Despite an operation to stop the bleeding, the side of her brain that controlled speech was damaged, as well as the coordination in her right hand. "All those nerves are interconnected." Finally he said, "She needs love and patience. So try and be good." After that, I didn't ask any more questions.

Within a week, a huge woman arrived at our house named Darlene McGinty. She marched into the living room like a five-star general. "Drill, drill, drill," she told my mother, "and you will learn to speak again." She'd worked with soldiers who'd been brain-damaged in Vietnam. We called her Ginty. Sometimes I'd watch her work with my mother. They sat at the kitchen table, Ginty in her heavy fisherman's sweater, Mother in her blue robe. Ginty began with the letter A. "Look at it and say 'Ahhh,' " she told my mother. "Look away and say it. Now write it." And they'd drill, drill, drill. Eventually, they put two or three letters together. B-a-t or c-a-t. Each letter from A to Z was a struggle. To form a word, to smooth it, was almost impossible. This went on for months. For the most part, I stayed out of Mother and Ginty's way.

"I've done all I can, Mr. Baskowitz," Ginty eventually told Dad. "She's on her own now."

Mother developed a set of expressions to use for everyday life. "I like that," or "It is awful." But she would never be fluent. To emphasize a point, she'd gesture with her hands, while struggling constantly to speak, to find the right words. But sometimes it proved too difficult. "I can't get it," she'd say, shaking her head in frustration. And then, despite her protests, we would help, say the words for her.

At first, her friends stopped by to visit. Some of them acted pained and self-conscious, others overly enthusiastic. "Oh, Franny, how wonderful you look. How well you're doing," they'd gush, even though my mother's face was puffy and she could only nod back at them. Then they'd stay a few minutes and rush off in a flurry of apologies. "There are people who can't handle being around someone who's handicapped. They just don't have the patience," Aunt Dorothy said. No one ever admitted that some people just don't care, that they're selfish, too wrapped up in themselves to bother. But that's what I kept thinking as I watched my parents' world shrink.

One night I was impatient with Mother over something and I screamed at her at the dinner table. Yanking me out of my chair, my father slapped me, not once, but over and over, until my mother and Merlie made him stop. "I don't feel sorry for you. I hate you. I wish you were dead," I whispered into my pillow that night. Why did this happen to us, I kept asking myself, somehow blaming her. Yet, all along, in the back of my mind, I remembered the way I acted the night she got sick.

Two years later, my father died of a heart attack in an elevator going up to his office. Even though he and I had some rough moments because of my mother, I loved him so much—everybody did. I try not to dwell on it. But little things remind me of him at odd moments: a whiff of his after-shave in a department store, or the smell of barbeque ribs in the neighborhood, and certain expressions that he liked to use: "Don't get a lackadaisical attitude," or "Look at things logically."

"Your father did her talking for her," said Aunt Dorothy. "Now we have to do it."

You do it, I remember thinking, but I didn't say anything. I was only twelve, in seventh grade at a new school. I had my own problems. For starters, I was ashamed to bring my friends over to play. The one time I brought someone home, my mother started plying her with questions in a slow, incoherent way. As I watched the girl's expression turn from confusion to pity, I vowed never to bring another person to my house.

I still remember the days when my mother was normal. That's what makes her condition so hard to accept now. I want her to be the same busy lady who used to lean over my bed and whisper "Good night, sleep tight," her hair soft on my arm, her eyelashes tickling my cheek in a butterfly kiss. Merlie's not bothered by Mother's halting speech and abrupt mannerisms because she doesn't remember her very well the other way. But I'll never get used to it. Neither will my Aunt Dorothy. Once, when Mother left the room, Aunt Dorothy said, "Franny used to be so articulate. She had an answer for everything." She still does. "This is a mess." "Stop." "Oh, Roxie." Anger and disappointment—all in one-syllable words.

2

The Sterns' house has become my safety zone. When I was small, I hid in a tree house; now I escape to Glo's. Despite Mother's protests, Glo's the best thing that's happened since we moved to this block. But it took us a long time to become friends. During most of junior high, she hardly ever spoke to me. In fact, she was the type who took fiendish delight in playing tricks on everyone in the class, especially me, the new girl. My first week at Bannister Prep, she and her friends took my homeroom desk and stuck it out in the hall. And even though I got to know some of the other kids, I always admired Glo, longed for her friendship. For one thing, she's wonderful to look at. She has a delicate, angelic face, framed by thick, curly blond hair. Sometimes all I'm aware of are her eyes, cobalt-blue and round as saucers. She has a way of looking at you intently, as if you're the most important person in the world. I used to watch her racing through the halls of Bannister Prep with her hair flying. She was like a comet blazing across the sky.

Finally there's her laugh, surprisingly loud and boister-

ous, coming from someone so small. Nobody laughs like
Glo. At least, that's what I thought, until I met her
mother. First their shoulders begin shaking; then they
fling their heads back and throw their whole bodies into
it. A laugh like that makes me want to say something
funny, just to watch their reaction.

When we moved to Hickory Lane, there was a definite
neighborhood clique. Right after the moving truck
pulled away, Mrs. Stern sent her chauffeur over with
some Godiva chocolates, but Glo rode by on her bicycle
and didn't even wave. At school, Glo and her friend
Buffy Marks stuck to each other like burrs. Then last
April, at the beginning of spring break, it snowed, a
terrible, record-breaking blizzard that blanketed the
neighborhood and made driving impossible. Buffy Marks
was in Sarasota with her parents. Practically everyone
from school was on vacation except Glo and me. My
mother doesn't travel anymore, but Glo stayed home
because she'd fallen off her bike and broken her leg. It
served her right, as far as I was concerned. That's when
my mother suggested, "Why don't you go visit that girl."
She pointed up the street. "In your class."

"No way. She hates me."

"Oh, Roxie." My mother gave me a raised-eyebrow
look and pressed her lips together, which never fails to
make me feel like some sort of misfit. True, I saw myself
as a social retard at Bannister Prep, but Glo Stern was just
the sort to confirm my opinion. Still, rather than admit
this to Mother, I zipped myself into a down jacket,
tugged on my snow boots, and trundled through the icy
street to the Sterns'. The house stands high on a hill, a
three-story, wood-frame colonial painted lavender, with

deep-purple shutters and a yellow door. I slipped and slid all the way up the long, steep driveway, vowing that if Glo wasn't friendly, I would go home and make up a good story. I had this fantasy that a butler would answer the door, usher me into a paneled library, and then Glo would refuse to come downstairs. Halfway up the hill, I heard someone pounding on the second-story window. Glo pushed up the window and yelled, "Are you going to take all day?" By the time I'd made it to the porch, Glo was at the door, wearing a white quilted robe decorated with red hearts. The cast poking through her robe looked as if someone had written graffiti all over it. I shoved the tin of cookies my mother made me bring into her hands. Then I stood there wondering what to do next. "Well, come on in," Glo said in that theatrical voice of hers. "I've never been so bored in my life." She clomped to the back of the house, pulling me with her. We passed through rooms painted every color of the rainbow, until we came to a small, emerald-green sitting room, where Glo sank into a mound of deep pillows on the couch and peered at me slyly as if waiting for me to say something interesting, to entertain her.

I glanced around. On the coffee table stood family photographs in ornate silver frames. I pointed to one of a young girl dressed in a ragged Indian cotton dress, her long blond hair strewn with flowers. She was waving a tambourine and gazing wistfully into space. "Who's that?"

Glo picked up the picture and set it back down. "Oh, that's my mother at a peace rally when she was sixteen."

"She looks like a hippie," I remarked, and immediately felt I'd said the wrong thing.

"She was—sort of," said Glo. "Dad calls her 'the for-mer flower child.' That picture was taken on the day he met her. He thought she was a homeless waif and took her out to Tony's for a fancy Italian dinner."

"How romantic."

"It was," Glo said, laughing. "He wanted to rescue her. But the joke was on him. She turned out to be the daughter of his father's partner."

"You mean they'd never met?"

"Dad's ten years older than Mother. He hadn't noticed her before. Then three months later they got married. She wasn't even out of high school."

"We're practically the same age as she was—*now*. I can't imagine being married at sixteen." I was shocked and impressed.

"Mother thinks she was too young," said Glo. "She's always telling me to wait until I've graduated from col-lege."

"All I want to do is get through Bannister Prep," I said.

Glo leaned toward me. "I'm going to have many lovers before I settle down." This was the most sophis-ticated thing I'd ever heard. She took a cigarette out of a silver case, lit it expertly, and started puffing away. Then, sputtering smoke and coughing, she said, "Aren't you?"

"I don't know. I just don't want to end up like my mother." Pretty soon I was telling her all about my family, and we spent the rest of the afternoon sharing secrets and gossiping. I knew I'd made it when she asked me to sign her cast and come back the next day.

3

"Let's take our positions," says Glo. Her Friday-night caper promised to keep my mind off the fact that I'd left my mother painting the front hall by herself. So Glo and I crouch on the second-floor landing, to peer downstairs through the railing. There her sister Irene's date, Sheldon Shapiro, struggles to make polite conversation with Mr. Stern.

"How're you doin'?" drawls Sheldon, running his finger through black hair that is slicked back like a gangster's from the thirties. We call Irene "the Princess" because she considers herself royalty. Her favorite song is "Someday My Prince Will Come." Most of her dates are eligible for the title, but not this one, in his tight rented tux, shiny as a wet suit.

"All he's missing are some goggles and fins," I say to Glo.

"Is he a total loser, or what? I've got to save Dad from this torture." Before I can stop her, Glo pulls off a dirty sneaker and flips it over the banister. The shoe lands on

16

Mr. Stern's foot at precisely the same moment that the Princess emerges from her dressing room to begin her royal descent. A strong odor of Giorgio precedes her. "What an incredible stench!" Glo holds her nose and dives forward on the rug, pulling me with her. She rolls around, hysterical, and I bury my face in the thick shag, trying to control myself. After all, the Princess isn't my sister. I don't want to tangle with her. There's no doubt she'll retaliate. As she sweeps by in a shimmering cloud of red net and sequins, she jabs Glo in the ribs with the silver point of her shoe. This produces an indignant howl, but the Princess keeps right on going, smiling radiantly in Sheldon's direction.

When Irene slips her arms with perfect precision into her mother's mink jacket, an odd feeling comes over me. Envy, awe? Whatever it is, my chest tightens and I catch my breath. The Princess dashes off to spend a glamorous evening with Sheldon, even if he is more Frog than Prince, while the two little mice stay home for another big night of rented rock videos.

Glo thinks it's horrible to be fifteen—old enough to wear a bra and get your period, but too young to drive or go out with boys who do. Even if some girls in our class date, neither the Sterns nor my mother allow it.

"We lead a sheltered life," I sigh dramatically, secretly glad Glo and I haven't had the chance anyway. We're not exactly overdeveloped for our age.

"What?" says Glo. "How can you say that? We're about to experience major child abuse." She points at Mr. Stern, who glares up at us, waving her sneaker, which from here resembles a flapping tongue. "He's not amused," remarks Glo. "Let's move out quick." Then she adds in a whisper, "But keep quiet. My mother's in bed."

"You're kidding? It's only seven."

For a moment Glo, who's usually in a continuous state of hyperactivity, goes perfectly still. "Oh," she says slowly, "she doesn't feel very well." Then she grabs my hand and we scramble up to the third floor, collapsing on the window seat, out of breath. "Did you catch Sheldon's face when he saw Irene? He was practically drooling." Glo snorts. "I feel sorry for the poor sap. He's about to become another victim."

"Do you remember the time she slammed the front door in Tommy Turner's face just as he was trying to kiss her good night?" I remind Glo. We double over again.

"I don't think old Sheldon has much of a chance either." Clutching Raggedy Andy, Glo presses her lips together and makes a loud smacking sound. "Kiss me, you fool." Then she rolls off the seat and lands on the floor, with her arms outstretched. "Oh, rats! If only I had a real boy to practice on. Hmmmmm . . . wonder what Tony Sansone's doing tonight?" This speculation is accompanied by a wink and a leer. Tony turned up at Bannister last year on a scholarship. The girls in our class practically faint when he goes by, especially Glo.

"Stick to dolls and stuffed animals," I say, throwing a pillow on her head. "There's no hope for you." Strange, Glo's thinking about Tony Sansone, while I'm wondering what's in the fridge. "Do you think there's any leftover ice-cream pie?"

"I might be hopeless," remarks Glo, "but you're completely dense. Come on. We might as well stuff ourselves. What else can we do?"

4

It's only six-thirty Saturday morning, but I can't sleep anymore. Sunlight streams in my eyes as if every ray in the Midwest is aimed at me. Glo's used to this early-morning onslaught and snoozes right through it. But at daybreak I'm awake. Yawning and rubbing my eyes, I wish the skylight was painted black. Mrs. Stern had them built in all the upstairs bedrooms because she believes in what she calls "the restorative powers of the rays."

It makes me smile to think of Mrs. Stern and the way she goes on about the sun. I've always believed the sun was magical, too. When I was little, I heard a fairy tale about a king who held a contest to find the perfect wife. He invited every maiden in the land to the palace and proclaimed: "Whosoever can stare longest into the sun shall become my queen." All the villagers gathered in the courtyard. Despite their taunting cries, the plain daughter of a humble woodchopper entered the contest. One by one, the other maidens dropped out. But the woodchopper's daughter, tears streaming down her cheeks, continued to peer into the fiery orb. Suddenly a flash of lightning transformed her into a great beauty. She won the king's hand as well as his heart. Of course, they lived happily ever after.

I wanted to be transformed too, so I'd stare into the sun until the light blinded me. Finally my mother warned me that I'd ruin my eyes. Maybe I've stopped staring into the sun, but at times I still wish I was someone else.

I can hear baby birds chirping and, in the distance, the steady hum of traffic. A crow struts on the window ledge and taps his beak on the glass. Glo sleeps soundly, her breath rising and falling in even rhythm. But I'm too restless to stay put. I slip quietly out of her room and creep downstairs to the second floor. The Sterns' bedroom door stands slightly ajar. As I tiptoe past, I see Mr. Stern in his business suit, sitting on the edge of the bed, leaning over his wife. Her tangled hair spills out over the pillow, and her eyes are closed. He's whispering, "Maggie, Maggie," as she shakes her head no. His voice sounds urgent. Transfixed, I stop at the door. Just then, Mr. Stern glances up and with a brusque gesture motions me away. I scurry past, my heart pounding. I didn't mean to be rude, but how can I explain my presence there? I hurry back up the stairs, panting, ashamed.

The Sterns seem so unreal, like characters out of a romantic novel. And I'm not sure where I stand with them, if they even approve of me. Despite Mrs. Stern's eccentric behavior and Glo's frequent pranks, no one could call this household casual. It's almost old-fashioned, in the sense that meals are served by Charles, who doubles as a chauffeur. One knocks before entering rooms, and dresses for dinner. Glo and Irene curtsy when company comes, and stand until adults are seated. I could write a book on manners from observing them. My mother doesn't give me that kind of information. Around the Stern household, a breach in etiquette is right up there with being boring.

Glo wakes up with a start. "What's wrong? You look like you've seen a ghost."

"Not quite. Your father thinks I'm a Peeping Tom."

"What do you mean?" She presses forward in bed and gives me a funny look.

"It's just that I happened to be passing their bedroom, and I saw your father bent over your mother, whispering to her. It was intense!"

"Did you hear what he was saying? Was my mother out of it?"

Out of it? What a strange way of putting it. "I think she was awake, but her eyes were closed. They looked like Scarlet O'Hara and Rhett Butler, especially your father."

"Just forget about it." Glo flings back the covers. Despite the large quantities of sweet things we both consumed last night, she's dainty as Tinker Bell in her pink silk pajamas. My stomach, however, has expanded like a blowfish.

We dress without saying much and go down to eat. Mrs. Stern's door is closed now, and she doesn't appear for breakfast. Glo takes a spoonful of scrambled eggs served in a silver dish. As soon as I gulp down my orange juice, I hop up. "Listen, I have to scoot." This time I've definitely overstayed my welcome. "Call you later."

Glo puts her hand on my arm. Her fingers, long and

slender, feel cold on my skin. "Can I come with you?" she asks in a small voice.

"But we hardly ever go to my house," I say, surprised.

Before she has a chance to answer, Toby, the housekeeper, carries in a white wicker tray. On it sit a pot of coffee and a bottle of aspirin. "Take this up to your mother. She wants to speak to you." Glo rolls her eyes and groans.

From somewhere upstairs, I hear the Princess practicing her scales. "Do re mi fa so la ti do," she trills in her operatic voice. Irene's supposed to have the best voice in the school and takes private lessons from a singing coach. Suddenly she hits a false note. "Sounds like the mating call of two pieces of chalk on a blackboard," I say to Glo. We burst out laughing, the tension broken.

"See ya," says Glo, taking the tray from Toby to go upstairs for her talk with Maggie.

5

For once, it's a relief to go home. I race through the garage into the back door to find my mother in her terry-cloth robe frying bacon and drinking coffee with my Aunt Dorothy. She always makes twelve cups, as if she's expecting the whole neighborhood, but Dorothy's her only customer. Mother gestures hello, moving her mouth in that deliberate way of hers before she speaks. "You're home"—she pauses to find the right word— "now . . . I mean soon." There's no trace of anger in her voice. I guess she's not holding last night against me, but then she never shows much emotion. It's part of her "keep up a good front" attitude.

"Early," I correct. "It got kind of sticky around there."

She nods and flips the bacon over. "So, what happened?" asks Aunt Dorothy. The Stern household never ceases to fascinate her. She refers to them as the Royals. My mother doesn't approve of people who live too extravagantly or spoil their children. But my aunt loves to hear all the gory details. "Better than watching *Dynasty*."

Still, Mother takes it all in. Even though I'm upset about what went on at the Sterns', I keep my thoughts to myself.

"Last night Irene went out with a real wimp," I say instead.

"Who?" Mother offers me a piece of bacon.

"I think his name was Sheldon Shapiro."

"I don't know him." There was a time when Mother knew practically every family in town. "It's my nature," she once said, "to be inquisitive. That's why I'm a social worker." Aunt Dorothy says people used to seek her out, go to her with their problems. But now Mother's the one with the problems.

"Well," she says, "I have to tell you this."

"What?"

"I don't know how to say it." She points to a name on a piece of paper.

"Herman Levin? Who's he?"

"He is a man."

"Obviously he's a man. What are you trying to say?"

She gestures in the air helplessly. "I can't . . ." She turns to my aunt. "Dorothy, you tell Roxie."

"What? Who's this Herman what's-his-name?"

"Your mother's going out on a date tonight with a very nice man."

"On a date?" What about my dad? Has she forgotten him already? "Who is he? Where did she find him?"

"She met him years ago," says Aunt Dorothy. "He just moved back into town. He used to be crazy about her in the old days."

"Does he know about her?"

"Oh, Roxie," says my mother sadly. "This is not nice." She shakes her head.

"I'm sorry. I didn't mean it that way," I say, "but I just don't get it."

Mother shakes her head again. "Oh, Roxie." Thrusting her hand in the air as if to say "I give up," she retreats from the kitchen.

"You get it. You just don't like it. Now be nice." Aunt Dorothy follows her out and leaves me standing there stunned, staring at the swinging door.

All kinds of weird thoughts race through my mind. He's after her money, he's crazy, he's a pervert. "Calm down," I tell myself, dialing Glo's number.

"Número uno Hickory Lane."

"You won't believe this. My mother's going out on a date."

"So, why not?" asks Glo.

"She can't date. How will she carry on a conversation with the guy?"

"The same way she does with anyone," says Glo. "I think it's great. What's with you?"

"I don't know," I mumble. "I've gotta go." It's hard to resist not slamming the phone down. No one understands how I feel—especially me. I can hear my dad's voice in my head. "Now let's look at this logically." But the way I feel has no logical explanation. Aunt Dorothy's right—Mother needs to go out more. Yet, even though things around here aren't so terrific, I've gotten used to the three of us—Mother, Merlie, and me. The idea of a stranger, some man I don't know, coming around, upsets me. And what if he can't handle Mother's handicap, the fact that she can't talk right or hold a normal conversation. I've seen the way people in stores or restaurants give her pitying looks when she stumbles through a sentence. I don't want to see her hurt. It's better that she stay home than go out and be humiliated. And maybe this Herman just wants to take out a rich widow. I've seen shows on TV like that . . . except we're not really rich . . . not like the Sterns. "Oh, I don't know," I say out loud again.

"What don't you know?" comes the voice of my sister, Merlie, who skips into the kitchen and starts munching on a piece of bacon.

"Did you hear Mother has a date?" I ask accusingly, as if it's Merlie's fault. My sister shrugs and chomps on her bacon. "I hope it's not a fiasco," I say. "She better not expect me to talk to him and act polite."

"Mother wants me to answer the front door," Merlie says proudly.

"All dressed up in your little yellow organdy dress, no doubt. This is the absolute pits."

Somewhere out in the street, a car honks. Merlie pulls back the curtains to take a look. "Time for my tennis lesson. Remind Mother to pick me up. It's her turn to do car pool," she says. I shrug. It's irritating the way nothing ever bothers Merlie. Maybe it's because she's only eleven. "Just remind her for me, Roxie, okay?"

The horn blasts again. Merlie grabs her racket from the pantry and dashes out. I watch her. Even from the back, she looks bouncy and cheerful, her pleated skirt unfolding behind her like a Japanese fan.

6

Monday morning. Two days after Mother's big date. Buffy Marks, Glo, and I wait at the corner for the school bus. When Charles, the Sterns' chauffeur, is late for work, Glo rides the bus. "With the peasants," she jokes. Irene shoots by in her red Corvette but doesn't even wave.

The cherry trees are in blossom and purple iris line the gray stone walk leading to the bus stop. I stand shivering in the cold April air. Ignoring Mother's advice, I refused to wear a sweater. Buffy's cocker spaniel, who follows her everywhere, prances at our feet, biting our socks. Buffy's real name is Martha, but she insists that we use her nickname, which is the same as the dog's. She has a thing for cocker spaniels. Instead of taking notes in class, she draws pictures of animals. Cats, horses, dogs—they all come out the same, with floppy ears, bushy tails, and long, spotted bodies. Buffy, with her wide, sad eyes and freckles, looks a lot like a cocker spaniel, too. Her parents are best friends with the Sterns. Buffy's claim to fame is that she's adopted. She's also Glo's devoted slave. But

27

now that Glo and I are best friends, I think she feels a little left out. "Sometimes," Glo says, "Buffy is boring."

"Did you read in the paper about the man who left his dog $100,000?" says Buffy.

"So, how was your mother's date?" asks Glo, ignoring her. Her cheeks are flushed pink from the wind, her hair golden in the morning sun. She's wearing her navy-blue Bannister blazer and new patent-leather flats with white stockings. Next to Glo, I must look like a bag lady in my oversized shirt and patched jeans.

"He was all right, I guess. But I only saw him from the back as they walked to the car."

"You mean you didn't check him out? I would have been there giving him the third degree," says Glo.

"I refused to come downstairs when Mother called me. But good old Merlie answered the door, all dressed up in her best party dress." I don't mention the fact that, once past the front door, Mother's date waded through paint-splattered plastic, buckets, and brushes, while I crossed my fingers that the mess would discourage him.

"Well, what did she say when she got home?" Glo persists.

"Not much. I waited up for her. They came back early enough and stayed downstairs for a while. I flushed the toilet about eight times to let her know I was still awake."

"Sounds like something my dad would do," says Glo. "Is she going out with him again?"

"I guess so. At least, that's what she told my aunt over the phone."

"Great," says Glo. I give her a dirty look. She seems to be getting some kind of perverse pleasure out of this.

"My parents ought to get a divorce," announces Buffy in her blunt, flat voice. "All they do is yell at each other. I don't know why they can't get along." She bends down and starts nuzzling her dog, crooning to him in baby talk.

"Here she goes again," says Glo, just as the striped blue-and-white Bannister bus rounds the corner and stops way ahead of us. Glo motions the driver to back up, but he doesn't budge. "He must not know who you are," I say, running forward to climb aboard. All three of us squeeze into the front seat, giggling.

"Let's see your algebra homework," orders Glo, dropping the subject of parents to get on with more important business. We start comparing our math sheets. Glo copies two problems off my paper.

"I don't understand the second question," whines Buffy.

"Just multiply by the square root," I explain. After repeating this three times to her and Glo, I give up. "There's too much racket on this bus to concentrate. Ask Mr. Dobbs before class."

"We're not all math wizards like you," says Glo, tapping me lightly on the head with her book. Although I don't mind giving her the answers, it bothers me that she never finishes her work.

"I don't know how long you can get away with your lackadaisical attitude," I tell her. Glo gives me a quizzical look. "Never mind," I say. Using one of my dad's favorite sayings brings on a wave of sadness. I shut my eyes and let it pass.

The ride is long and noisy. Paper airplanes zoom over our heads, and from somewhere behind us comes a thumping noise. The commotion makes me edgy, but Glo loves it. "How can you stand this when you can ride to school in style?" I ask.

"It's embarrassing to be dropped off in a chauffeur-driven Cadillac," she says.

"Maybe so, but at least you're not bombarded with debris and abusive behavior for thirty minutes every morning."

"And guess who's getting on next?" Glo makes little kissing sounds.

The bus driver takes a sharp turn, and the bus lunges down a narrow street lined with three dilapidated farm-houses. The Sansone family, who run the gas station at the corner, live here. The bus grinds to a halt. Two dirty little boys, about four or five, race around the ragged front yard. They stop and eye the bus.

After much honking, the driver revs the motor and starts to take off. That's when Tony Sansone swaggers out, like a fighter ready to enter the ring. He's the only tenth-grader who's earned a Bannister letter jacket, which he never takes off. He dawdles for a moment with his brothers, tossing a ball back and forth, then nods over at us as if to signal he's ready. Everyone on the bus stares out at him. This is his routine.

"Come on, Tony, flex your muscles for us, and then get on the bus," yells the driver, who's not impressed. Even though I want to laugh at this remark, I don't dare. No one does. Tony's liable to fly off the handle. Once, when Harry Morgan told him he smelled like gasoline, Tony gave him a karate chop and held him down in a half nelson until Harry gave up.

As Tony saunters by, his arm brushes our seat. Glo lets out an audible sigh and pokes me.

"Hey, Tony, over here," calls John Lesser, his best friend.

Tony doesn't even know I exist, so I pretend he doesn't either and turn in the other direction. Glo laughs. "Admit it, Roxie. You think he's cute."

"Fair," I say, the way my mother does, slow and emphatically. "But you're out of control."

"He has amazing eyelids," Glo says, throwing her head back. "They're hooded."

"Hooded? How absolutely smashing," I remark, in my best Lady Di imitation. Then I sneak a look in his direction. He and John are whispering.

"Are you going to John Lesser's party Saturday night?" asks Buffy. "I got my invitation Saturday." She pulls a white card out of her grammar book. On it is stapled a piece of wilted lettuce.

" '*Lettuce* entertain you,' " I read out loud. " 'It *salad* of fun.' No, I'm not invited." I sniff as if it doesn't matter. Glo fidgets and exchanges funny looks with Buffy.

"You don't have to make faces at each other. I could care less."

"Not to worry, Roxie. Maggie will call Mrs. Lesser and make sure you're added to the list."

"I wouldn't go if you paid me."

"Don't be a grouch," says Glo. I sink down in the seat. My mother wasn't invited to the Martins' wedding reception, although Pat Martin was her best friend before she got sick. My Aunt Dorothy said, "There's only one thing worse than having to go to that party, and that's not being invited." "Who needs them?" my mother replied. She was too proud to act hurt. But I know I'll worry about the party, wonder why he left me out. When the bus finally stops in the school lot, John Lesser and I happen to get off at the same time.

"So what's up, Roxie?" he asks in his usual sociable way.

"As if you didn't know," I snort.

"Huh?" Then a look of understanding spreads over his face. He shuffles from his right foot to his left. John is one of the few good guys in our class. I'm almost sorry I've put him on the spot. But some impulse makes me go on. "I thought we were friends."

John's tall for his age, with big ears and a long, solemn face. Hunching over, he reminds me of an overgrown rabbit. "Gee, Roxie, I'm really sorry. My mother made out the list."

Feeling embarrassed, I say quickly, "Just forget it," and stalk off. For the rest of the day, I try to avoid him, but every time I turn a corner, there he is, giving me sheepish looks.

After school, the Sterns' chauffeur is waiting in front to drive Glo home. "Come with me," Glo says. "I hate getting into this big car alone."

"But I need permission to skip the bus."

"Forget that," Glo orders with a knowing look. "You ought to come over." If I don't go with her, will she accidentally on purpose forget to talk to Maggie about John's party?

Glo slides in front with Charles, and I'm stuck in the back seat alone. Charles is smoking a fat cigar and wears his chauffeur's cap cocked over his forehead. "You go on back with your friend," he tells her.

Glo flips herself backward and lands on the seat next to me. "If I sit in front, people might not know Charles is a chauffeur." Glo's really weird about things like that.

On the way to One Hickory, Charles stops at the cleaners, the grocery store, and the florist. He carries various items to the car ceremoniously, as if he's engaged in some important ritual. "Your bouquet, madam," he says to Glo, dumping the flowers on her lap.

Charles swings into the driveway tooting the horn, and parks. Glo insists on carrying everything inside. "You bring the cleaning," she says to me. "It makes me feel funny when Charles does all the errands. My mother should . . ." Then she stops in midsentence. "Let's see if Toby's made fresh cookies."

In the breakfast nook, Toby sets down a tray with two glasses of cherry Cool-Aid and a plateful of sugar cookies dripping with icing. "I love you, Toby," says Glo, hugging her. Toby's arms remain at her sides, her back stiff. Glo behaves as if Toby is her second parent, but Toby seems reserved with her, uncomfortable with Glo's bursts of affection. "Where's Mother?" Glo skips around Toby and pops a cookie in her mouth.

"Your mother is in the studio today," says Toby in her clipped Scottish accent.

The studio, off the Sterns' bedroom, is an upstairs porch that's been glassed in. "Wait a second." Glo knocks first and goes in. I hear some whispering, but I can't make out what they're saying. A moment later, Glo motions me inside. I wonder if I should ask Mrs. Stern how she's feeling, but she looks fine, perched on a high stool in front of a brightly colored canvas. Her hair snakes down her back in a long ponytail. Her face glistens in the sunlight as if she's polished her skin with Vaseline. She reminds me of a lovely white bird with a long neck and a crest of yellow feathers. In the background, Julio Iglesias warbles in broken English.

"How are you, Mrs. Stern?" I ask anyway.

Her smile turns into a frown. "I'm perfectly fine. Has Glo been fussing about me?"

My eyes meet Glo's. Her face is blank. "Well, no," I stammer, feeling as if I've stuck my foot in my mouth, but not sure how.

"Come over here and look at my new painting. I'd rather talk about that than the state of my health." Relieved by the change of subject, I squint at the picture. It seems to be a series of red and pink slashes. Stacked around the room are many paintings of various sizes, in vibrant shades of red, yellow, and black. I think she's been conducting Julio's music with her brush.

"That picture makes me think of a bonfire," I say. "That one of a sunrise. They're beautiful."

"The two things I can count on to make me feel wonderful," says Mrs. Stern, "are Julio's songs and the sun rising and setting every day." The brush slips out of her hand. For a moment she looks startled, as if she didn't realize she was holding it.

Glo bends down to pick it up. "What about me?" she asks. "You can count on me."

"Your father, too. I can always count on Ray." Then Mrs. Stern giggles. I smile back at her, not because anything strikes me as funny, but because I sense she expected some kind of response. "I'm dedicating this whole series of paintings to him," Mrs. Stern says, pointing to the stereo. "Sit down, darlings, and keep me company." It occurs to me that no one ever says "darling" like that except on TV.

Glo and I arrange ourselves on two of the huge brocaded pillows scattered around the room and listen to her enthuse about the sun. Not only do the words hold my attention, but also the rhythm of her voice, which is deep and melodious, like a folk singer's. She paces back and forth, her silk caftan swishing around her legs, her silver bracelets jingling.

"Maggie," says Glo, in a very serious voice, "you have to do us a very big favor."

Mrs. Stern focuses her full attention on us. Both Glo and her mother have the same intense look. "What is it, darling?" All of a sudden, I have the urge to stop Glo. But she rushes on to explain about the party. "Everybody's been invited but Roxie . . . Even Tony Sansone."

"Oh, dear, that's not good." I'm not sure how to take that. Does Mrs. Stern mean it's not good that I'm not invited or that Tony is? "That's not good at all," she repeats again as if I've just contracted a rare disease. "I'm sorry."

People are always saying "I'm sorry" to me. I hate it. I don't want to be pitied because my father's dead or because my mother's sick or because of anything else, especially because I haven't been invited to some stupid party. Tears well up in my eyes. "Excuse me. I have to go to the bathroom." Locking the door, I sink down on the cool white tile. Once in third grade a girl up the street had a birthday party. Most of the kids on the block had been invited; I wasn't. "Lucy hates me," I told my mother, crying. "You don't like everybody, either," Mother said. "Not being invited means everyone can't like everybody else." It bothers me that my mother isn't able to explain things like that anymore.

After a while I calm down. Back in the studio, Mrs. Stern is talking into the telephone. "Bobsie, I know the party's for our crowd, but Glo says that Tony, you know, the scholarship child, is invited." She pauses. "No, I don't know the mother well. It's Shakowitz."

"Baskowitz," says Glo.

"Yes, yes. Really so sad. She's the one who had the stroke, and then the father . . ." Her voice trails off. She glances at me, then averts her eyes. I feel my heart sink. "Oh, good," continues Mrs. Stern. "I'll pass the message on to Roxie. She'll be pleased. Bye-bye." I wonder why Mrs. Stern doesn't know my last name yet. Glo and I have been friends since last April. "All taken care of. Roxie, you're invited. It seems John's already given Bobsie the word."

Glo beams at her mother. "Thanks, Maggie."

A word-of-mouth invitation is better than nothing, but I still feel weird about it. My mother doesn't like asking anyone for favors, especially the Sterns. But if John really mentioned me to his mother, it would restore my faith in him.

7

Every Sunday night before I fall asleep, I tell myself that tomorrow's going to be the beginning of the best week I've ever had. I make deals with myself, invent ambitious schemes and crazy plans. My father always talked about goals and long-term planning. But I can't imagine what I'll be doing in a month or in a year. It's easier to take one day at a time. In bed, I compose a list: take perfect notes in history; memorize French vocabulary words; read one chapter of *Pride and Prejudice;* be nice to Mother. All fired up, I arrive at school Monday morning with clean hair, a coordinated outfit, pencils sharpened, and books in order. But somehow, by Thursday, I'm burnt out. It's too hard to keep the energy going, especially when a variety of annoying things happen along the way.

Obsessing about that stupid party all day last Monday blew the week right from the start. So now it's Thursday and my hair is dirty. I'm two lessons behind in French, and an English composition on Jane Austen is already overdue. No problem, I tell myself. My favorite class is about to begin, and for an hour I can completely space out. "Body Conditioning with Aerobics Eddie." This program was initiated by Mrs. Spencer, the headmistress, to be "innovative" and to give Aerobics Eddie, her nephew, a job. He's here to whip us into shape.

Eddie's about my height, 5'5", with a tight-muscled body and a long, thin face. As far as I can see, he's managed to eradicate body fat from his life altogether. He's so nimble, he actually ripples when he moves, like a Slinky slithering across the floor. Every Tuesday and Thursday during second period, the Hoppmeier Memorial Gym vibrates with pulsating rhythms and reeling bodies. "I mean, it's time to gyrate," Eddie begins, strutting about in a black leotard, with a red bandanna tied around his forehead and orange leg warmers pulled up to his knees. "Pretend you're a Cuisinart. Toss and tumble like a crazy salad." He turns on a Donna Summer tape, and fifty clumsy adolescents begin to lurch and leap around the room.

The entire junior varsity football team is here, sweating it out along with Glo, Buffy, and me. We volunteered to be Aerobics Eddie's guinea pigs. Reeling and whirling, flailing and floundering, we undulate nonstop for forty-five minutes. Amazingly enough, I'm in my element. Sometimes Eddie even brings me up front to demonstrate. My body moves in ways I've never dreamed possible. My balance is good, my mind a complete blank. My forehead, chin, arms, and legs, all my parts enter in the next movement, to the beat of the music. "Stagger and slump are not in our vocabulary. Don't forget to breathe," he booms over the music. "Heels down, heels down. Who wants to be sweet sixteen with flabby thighs? Light on your feet, boys," he tells the jocks. "What's with all this thumping?"

The first day of class, the football team appeared wearing tutus over their shorts. Then Eddie stretched out on the floor and started leading them in push-ups. Long after the last boy dropped in an exhausted heap, Eddie was bobbing up and down, singing with the music. "Now clean up your act," he told them. Since then, not one of them has given him a bit of trouble.

Glo balances precariously on her spindly legs and waves her arms. The music and Glo's movements are totally unsynchronized. Every few minutes, she collapses. "This is supposed to make me stronger," she says, "but instead it feels like I've pulled every muscle in my body."

"I think I'm going to die," says Buffy, panting. "This is worse than getting the flu." Tony Sansone concentrates on a series of deep knee bends in front of us. Glo concentrates on watching him. "He's my only incentive," she whispers.

John Lesser, tangled like a pretzel, uncurls himself and winks at me. "Good going, Roxie." Ever since our awkward exchange concerning the party, he seems to be making an extra effort to be nice.

"How do you manage?" asks Glo. "You're a natural, Roxie."

"It's about time I found something to excel in besides adding two and two. My luck, aerobics happens to be listed under 'alternative education.' "

"None of this false modesty," says Glo.

At the end of class, we run fifteen laps around the gym, and I'm not even tired. "You ought to try out for track," Eddie tells me after the bell rings. "You've got the endurance for it."

"Maybe I will," I say, wiping the perspiration off my forehead. But I don't tell him the reason I've never tried out. An image of ten little girls standing in a line flashes through my mind. They wait nervously to be chosen for relay teams. The one with the long black braids is picked last. Guess who that was? As far as I'm concerned, team sports are in the same category as tetanus shots and oatmeal.

"Listen, Roxie," Eddie says. "I'm only here for a few months. The board voted for one trial semester to appease Aunt Elvira. But if I could teach my technique to a few of you kids, you might be able to continue on your own after I leave."

"What about coaching the gym teachers?"

"Hah," he snorts. "Those jocks? All they're interested in is winning competitions." Eddie does a couple of quick leg stretches. "Look," he says, as I turn to go, "I'm teaching a class to the first- and second-graders. I could use some help. They're a wild bunch. Why don't you come over to the Primary School with me sometime and help out."

When Eddie smiles, his dimples crease and his whole face crinkles. He's smiling at me now, and I find myself grinning right back. "Little kids aren't my favorite species, but maybe I'll give it a try." Suddenly I feel terrific. No teacher's ever asked me to do anything besides keep quiet or turn in my homework on time. I've never been a team captain, a class officer, or even a room monitor. Once I was put in charge of cleanup after a Valentine's Day party, but somehow that didn't thrill me. "I know your routines already," I tell Eddie. "I really like what you're doing."

Eddie laughs. "I'm glad I've got at least one fan around here besides my Aunt Elvira." He bends over to collect his tapes. "Meet me here Monday morning during your lunch hour, and we'll go down to the Primary School together."

"It's a deal."

8

After the bus drops me off, I find Mother sitting in the living room with Harvey Rosenwald, her stockbroker, better known as the Mole on account of his beady eyes and tiny, pointed ears. In my opinion, he belongs in a hole underground. He's scrunched into the wing chair, with his briefcase open on his lap. Mother sits across from him in her beige linen suit, studying a long sheet of paper. I can tell by the way she's twirling her glasses that she's not pleased. The Mole gives me a toothy smile.

"Hello, Mr. Rosenwald," I say, offering my hand in my most polite manner.

"Well, now, how are you, Rochelle?" he wheezes, pumping my hand firmly. "Break any hearts lately?"

"Oh, thousands," I say. Remaining pleasant is going to be difficult.

"She's certainly growing into a fine young lady, Frances."

Mother nods, pointing to the couch. "Sit down, Roxie."

42

The last thing I need is a lecture on the stock market.
"I'm busy." I turn to go.

"Sit down," she repeats, and waves the paper at Harvey. "I don't like this. I told you, not this way."

"Now, Frances, maybe I misunderstood you," he says,
weakly. "I thought we decided not to sell those computer
stocks, to wait it out."

"No, no. You did understand me. You can't use that.
No!" she says, emphatically. Harvey Rosenwald has
made a mistake, but he's using her handicap to weasel out
of it. When it comes to business, Aunt Dorothy says
Mother's a genius. She takes a pencil from the table and
begins to mark the sheet. I know she's having trouble
writing because of her hand.

"Can I help?" I ask.

"Here, Roxie, write what I say." All her stocks have
been listed by Harvey in a typewritten column, with the
purchase price and monthly quotes. Three stocks, I notice,
have risen and fallen thirty points. She's scribbled something illegible next to them.

"Do you want me to write 'sell'?" I ask.

She nods. Harvey, crossing and uncrossing his stubby
legs, squints over at us as I try to follow her halting
directions. "You must do what I say. I know," she tells
Harvey.

"Of course you know, Frances, but . . ."

Mother holds up her hand to silence him. "No!" The
subject is closed. One thing about my mother, when she
makes up her mind, that's it. She can be very stubborn.
The Mole's getting frustrated. He's still blinking furi-

ously. Sometimes I feel the same way when she insists she's right and won't budge.

"You have to make things more clear," he says in a wheedling voice, unwilling to admit he's wrong. I recognize the tone; I'm an expert at it. I feel a flush of shame. My mother shouldn't have to take that stuff from anyone.

She hands him the list. "Sell these stocks. Buy IBM."

"IBM won't go up much more," warns Harvey, in a slow, nasal voice. "It's inflated already." He gives us a gloomy smile.

"We will see," my mother says firmly and stands up. "I know," she says almost to herself after Harvey burrows his way out. Then she collapses back on the chair and rests her head on her hand. But she doesn't break down. I've never seen her cry, not even when Dad died.

I stand and watch her for a moment. "Mother, I got a job today." Maybe that will cheer her up.

She looks puzzled. "What?"

"At school. I'm going to help with an exercise class for the little kids."

"Oh," Mother says, unimpressed, and picks up her balance sheet.

"Well, don't look so excited about it."

"What class? I don't see . . ." My mother was once named Social Worker of the Year. To her, leading an exercise class probably sounds like nothing. "You should study, not . . ." She bends up and down, imitating an exercise.

"Never mind," I tell her. "May I go now?" I'm already halfway up the stairs when I hear her say "Oh, Roxie," in an exasperated voice.

Merlie bumps into me on the landing and doesn't even say "Excuse me." Locked in my room, I start feeling like a brat. Always getting mad, causing a fight. But why can't my mother ever act proud of me? Why can't she just act normal?

I dial Glo's number. "Irene's social secretary," Glo answers.

"Surprise. This is an obscene phone call for you."

"The last ten have all been for Irene," says Glo. "She thinks she's Queen of Southwestern Bell."

"I'm coming over," I tell her. "This house is full of deranged people."

"One less if you leave," says Glo. "By the way, stay for dinner. Toby's cooking chicken pot pie." The only experience I've ever had with chicken pot pie came straight from the freezer, a Stouffer's frozen special. Seated meals at the Stern's can be wonderful productions —linen napkins, candles, and fancy food like escargots or fresh raspberries and chocolate mousse. The only problem is the pressure to make stimulating conversation. I have to be in the right mood, so I hesitate before answering. This pregnant pause doesn't slip past Glo. "Puh-lease, Roxie, it's so much nicer when you're here." How can it be nicer, I wonder, than it already is? But the fact that she really wants me there lifts my spirits, especially after that last exchange with my mother. And let's face it, Toby's chicken pot pie sounds better than our Thursday-night menu: boiled chicken and cabbage, an old family recipe that should have been left in Russia.

"Maybe if Irene isn't blow-drying her hair or memorizing 'Doe, a deer,' she'll take us shopping," says Glo, to tempt me further. "We have to prepare ourselves for John's party Saturday night." Then she hangs up.

Taking off, I cut through the Meyers' back yard and follow the creek to Glo's. There's not quite enough water to cover the large, round stones that line the creek bed. Hopping from stone to stone without getting my shoes wet is always a challenge. But right away a big rock tilts under my weight, and I lose my balance. I guess I'm not paying attention. The back lawns of Hickory Lane spread before me in long stretches of green, marked with the deep shadows of hickory trees just beginning to flower. In the autumn, Merlie and I collect the smooth-shelled nuts to fill straw baskets that sit near our fireplace. My sneakers are sopping by the time I reach Glo's. I sink down on her porch steps to tug them off. An aroma of freshly baked pie is wafting out from the kitchen window. The mellow tones of Julio Iglesias mingle with shrill voices coming from upstairs.

"I'm busy, twit. Tell Charles to drive you," shrieks Irene. "I don't need to cart you and that ratty mess around."

"You're supposed to drive me if I need to go somewhere," Glo yells back. "That was the deal when they bought you a car."

"Only in emergencies," snaps Irene.

What did I hear Irene say? "I don't need to cart you and that ratty mess around." Is she talking about me? What did she mean by that? My head is spinning; I can't move from the steps. Why did Irene say that? Sometimes Mr. Stern makes a big deal about how tidy and pretty Irene and Glo are, as if this condition is a state of grace, the mark of some special accomplishment. But what's wrong with me? Just because I prefer sweat clothes to monogrammed sweaters . . . Irene's and Glo's voices rise and fall, gradually fading out. "Mother!" comes a last wail from Irene.

Pretty soon she slams out the back door, brandishing her keys, with Glo following right behind, a triumphant grin on her face. The Princess beams when she spots me, as if I'm her long-lost friend. "Roxie, you cute thing," she says, her voice sticky as molasses. "Do you and Glo really need to go to Saks to buy makeup? Aren't you beautiful enough without painting your face?"

"Are you speaking to me, the ratty mess?" I'm tempted to ask, but I can't bring myself to do it.

"Irene," says Glo. "You only have twenty-four tubes of lipstick and eye shadow. Perhaps you could replenish your supply as well." Irene gives her a scalding look. "Grab your shoes, Roxie." So, off we go to the shopping center, Glo and I pressed together in the tiny back seat of the Corvette, Irene and her purse in the front. The top's down, the radio's blaring, and I feel as if everyone on the road must be staring at us enviously.

Irene swerves into the parking lot and jolts to a halt about a block from the store. "You could have dropped us off at the entrance," complains Glo.

"You know I always park away from other cars, to protect my car from getting dents. Consider yourself lucky to be here at all."

As Glo and I race toward the store, I find myself blurting, "What did Irene mean when she called me a ratty mess?" Glo stops dead in her tracks and gives me her wide-eyed, innocent look. "I heard her say it," I persist.

"It's just something ridiculous," Glo says. "Not to worry."

"What do you mean?" I say, folding my arms and holding my ground.

"Look, if I tell you, swear you won't get upset."

"I'm already upset."

"Okay, okay." She can't even look me in the eye.

"It's just that when you and I first became friends my father didn't like you. He told us he thought you looked sloppy."

"What?" I practically scream, feeling a tightness in my chest. "Sloppy?"

"Well, you know what a nut he is about neatness. And you're not exactly a candidate for Miss Well-Groomed of the Year."

True, clothes and haircuts take last place on my list of priorities. But even though my sneakers are untied and caked with creek mud, there's nothing improper about the way I look. "Glo . . ."

"Never mind. Now that Dad's gotten to know you, he doesn't talk that way anymore. Forget it!" She grabs my hand and drags me with her. I allow myself to be pulled along, trying to calm down, past the revolving doors, through the shoe department, until we reach the Clinique section, Glo's favorite makeup counter.

"My lips are absolutely throbbing with excitement," says Glo, pointing to the rows of bright pinks, reds, and oranges that gleam like polished fruit in the case. The saleswoman, dressed in a white jacket as if she's a doctor, gives us a glossy smile. "This is from our new line.

Heartbreak Red." She touches her lips, which look bruised with color. Glo elbows me to get into the act. But I'm too upset to say anything.

The clinician flaps her false eyelashes at me. "Maybe you don't like the color."

"No," says Glo. "It's the idea of Heartbreak. Scarlet Shame and Flaming Flamingo are out, too." She scrutinizes the case. "What we need are your testers and some Kleenex.

"Does this contain liquor?" Glo says, picking up Blushing Brandy. "My mouth is watering already." Her laugh rings out. When she actually produces a smile from the saleswoman, I give in and smile, too. Rosy Rapture, Frantic Fuchsia, Tahiti Spice, Prize Poppy, and Pink Promise. Glo tries them all. Puckering and blotting, she can practice kissing Kleenex for hours. "This is for Tony. *Te amo,*" declares Glo, puckering her lips and practically devouring the piece of Kleenex. "I have a passion for red." She finally decides on three tubes of Jazzy Magenta. Glo never buys one of anything. I'm feeling a little better, watching her clown around. So I settle for Ardent Rose and some green eye shadow, even though I won't ever use them. I go along with these makeup splurges to please Glo.

Just as we're about to go through the glass doors, I hear a familiar voice, loud and insistent, behind me. "No, I don't want that." It's my mother. Franny Baskowitz in the flesh.

Oh, no, I think.

"There's your mother," says Glo, who's spotted her, too. No way I can avoid her now. "Hi, Aunt Frances," says Glo, cheerily. She has a habit of adopting the whole world.

"Glo," says Mother, nodding. Right away I notice cake crumbs are stuck on her lip. After the operation, she lost all sensation on the left side of her mouth. When food dribbles down, she can't feel it.

"Hi, Mother." I can barely look at her, I feel so embarrassed.

Mother looks me up and down. "Oh, Roxie, your hair." She delivers this line with such force that one would think my hair is a rat's nest. Not you, too. What am I, a disaster area? Then she shakes her head and turns back to the saleswoman. She indicates some unspecified purse behind the counter. "That is the one," Mother says. "Brown. There." The saleswoman holds up three likely choices. My mother takes the one with the tortoise-shell handle. "Is it"—she pauses to find the right word—

"Leather?" the lady suggests.

"No, no." Mother shakes her head and fingers the price tag.

"Oh, you mean is it on sale," the saleslady says impatiently.

My mother stands very straight and holds her hand up like a policeman stopping traffic. "I will say it." Glo stares at her wide-eyed. I feel pressure building up in my head. I want to disappear. I wonder if everyone around us is watching, listening to her try to talk. She struggles a few more times and finally says, "Is this on sale?"

By now the lady is indignant. "Yes," she says, in a huffy voice. "That is what I've been trying to tell you." But my mother is undaunted. She tries to talk everywhere she goes, refusing to be concerned if people stare at her. Ginty used to say, "The more you talk, the better you will get. Don't bother about what other people think." But *I'm* bothered.

"Can't you just let yourself be helped once in a while?" I mumble, while the saleslady is ringing up the sale. "Do you have to take up so much time?"

"I can't help it, Roxie." She wags her finger at me. "That is all."

"We've got to dash," says Glo. "The Princess is waiting."

"I'm eating at the Sterns'." With that, I escape from Saks and Mother as quickly as possible.

"Your mother's really neat," says Glo. "You shouldn't be so hard on her."

"Easy for you to say. You don't live with her," I tell Glo. But I feel guilty for acting so nasty again.

Out in front, Irene is tapping her long fingernails impatiently on the dash. "Took you long enough."

"Let me drive, Irene. Please," begs Glo. She pulls out a tube of Jazzy Magenta. "Look, I bought this for you for being such a sweetie."

Irene checks it out, then drops the lipstick in her pocket. "The answer's still no."

Glo's eyes narrow and take on a dangerous glint. "If you don't turn the wheel over to me right now, Miss High-and-Mighty, I'm going to show Dad the hole you and your stupid friends burned in the Persian rug."

"You can't prove a thing." But Irene's lips are twitching.

"And then I'll tell him to take a peek under your bed.

You've stuffed enough junk under there to hold a rummage sale."

And you call me a mess, I'm tempted to interject. Nothing upsets Mr. Stern more than disorder. He probably has drawer check once a month.

"Okay, okay, you win. But only for a mile down Clayton Road. You are really a . . ."

"Now, now. No vulgarity in front of my friend."

"Hah," snorts the Princess.

Grudgingly, she moves over to let her sister in. It takes Glo a minute or two to start the car. "Turn the key on, not the windshield wipers, you numskull," says Irene. Glo releases the emergency break, and the car jerks forward.

"I'm going to freak," I tell her. "I didn't know you could drive."

"Just hold on to your hat," says Glo. With her chin jutting forward, her hands practically glued to the steering wheel, Glo maneuvers the car out of the shopping center at about two miles an hour. I feel as if we're doing eighty.

"Don't drive in the middle of the road," Irene warns her. After about two blocks, Irene says, "That's enough. Pull over and let me drive before Roxie and I have heart attacks." For once, I'm in complete agreement with her.

Glo turns the car over to her sister without a peep. I pat her on the back. "Good going. Next week you'll be ready for the Demolition Derby."

9

That night, before dinner at the Sterns', I scrub my face until it's shiny and run the comb through my hair a dozen times. Why does Mr. Stern think I'm sloppy? I may not look as if I've just stepped out of *Vogue*, but I didn't drag in from the gutter either. When Glo and I go into the dining room, he and Irene are sitting at the end of the table, deep in conversation. Looking at them, I think they make a perfect picture, father and daughter, their faces softly lit by candlelight, their heads close together. I feel a lump in my throat, that twinge of envy that sometimes comes over me when I'm here.

"That's great, baby, just great," Mr. Stern is saying to Irene.

"What?" asks Glo, plopping in her seat on the opposite side.

"Your sister's the lead in the spring play, Maria in *The Sound of Music*. Isn't that marvelous?"

"Oh, that," says Glo indifferently, fiddling with her spoon. She presses the handle with her thumb. The spoon flips off the table, bouncing on the hardwood floor.

"Really, Glo," says Mr. Stern. "Can't you sit at the table without fidgeting?"

Irene fixes her cool gaze on me. "I've already played Lady Macbeth and the Virgin Mary."

"You ought to make a great nun," says Glo, kicking me under the table. To try not to laugh, I stare at the crystal chandelier, then down at the lace-edged napkin and at the red tulips drooping in the centerpiece. Irene and Mr. Stern resume their conversation, their voices low, clearly excluding us. Glo scowls into her plate. I wonder where Mrs. Stern is. Is she sick again? My stomach rumbles as I look around for the rolls. There's no food on the table yet, so I assume we're waiting for Glo's mother. As if she's read my mind, Irene says in an icy tone, "Is Mother coming down for dinner tonight, or doesn't she feel well again?"

"Darlings," says Mrs. Stern from the doorway, her arms outstretched in an Isadora Duncan pose. She weaves her way to the table.

Mr. Stern rises stiffly and pulls out her chair. "Nice of you to join us," he says. But if Mrs. Stern catches his sarcasm, she doesn't let on. In fact, she doesn't even glance in his direction. Her hair is piled on her head, with bobby pins that spill off one by one during the soup course, until her blond curls fall in total disarray around her face. She's wearing a Chinese robe held together by a safety pin. It flips open every now and then, revealing bare skin which I try not to notice. Speaking of sloppy, Mr. Stern must be having a fit! Whenever Irene or Glo says anything, she laughs, even when it's not particularly funny. She keeps ringing the little silver bell, and Charles scurries in and out, clearing the soup bowls, pouring wine, making funny faces at Glo and me.

Pretty soon we all start giggling over nothing. "Ladies! Control yourselves!" blusters Mr. Stern. We shut up immediately. After a small lull, he clears his throat. "I've been reading a book about body language. The author can judge a man's character, size him up in a minute, just by watching the way he sits or holds his head."

Glo says, "That sounds impossible."

Mr. Stern directs his cool gaze at me. "Well, I'll give you an example. See the way Roxie's holding her hands in a fist? That's a dead giveaway."

"For what?" asks Irene.

"I can tell she's nervous," Mr. Stern says. "You don't mind my pointing that out, do you, Roxie?"

I uncurl my fingers and thrust my hands in my lap. Completely flustered, I try to think of something clever to say back, but nothing comes. On top of everything else, now he probably thinks I'm boring.

"More wine, please," Mrs. Stern tells Charles, who's moving around the table, setting down salad plates.

Glo fingers her roll and picks at a tomato. Irene takes dainty bites. While Mrs. Stern sips her wine, Mr. Stern glowers. Still tongue-tied, I focus on what's left of my salad, certain it's my fault dinner's turned into such a disaster.

During the chicken-pot-pie course, Glo practically turns green, bolts up, and dashes out of the dining room. "Where's she racing off to?" asks Mr. Stern.

"She reacts to the least little thing," says Irene in her

know-it-all voice. The Princess addresses this comment to me, as if I'm expected to confirm it. I glare back. Who wouldn't react to all this tension?

"Hmm . . . Is she ill?" asks Maggie in a vague voice, as if she's talking about the weather.

"Don't be ridiculous," Mr. Stern retorts. "She's just high-strung, like you."

"Really, Ray," says Mrs. Stern, raising her eyes to his for the first time. She gives him an imploring look. "I'm worried about her."

"All right, all right. I'll go see what's the matter." Quickly he wipes his mouth with his napkin, pushes back his chair, and goes striding out.

All this time, Irene is sitting with her spine arched conspicuously away from her chair back, as if she's totally aloof from this little exchange. "I think I'll have my dessert later," she says with a majestic shrug, and leaves. As for me, I just want to go home. Lately, every time I come around here, some crisis erupts.

Mrs. Stern smiles apologetically. "I don't know what's gotten into Glo lately. You're her best friend, Roxie. Why is she so difficult? She used to be such an angel."

"It's probably growing pains," I offer. That seems noncommittal enough.

"Maybe she needs some sun," says Mrs. Stern. "She might be suffering from sun deprivation." She swirls the wine in her goblet. A few red drops spill over the edge and stain the white cloth, but she doesn't seem to notice. Maybe she doesn't care. Is everyone around here crazy, I wonder, or is it me?

"Shall I clear the table?" I suggest, eager to get away.

"No, no, you go on," says Mrs. Stern. "I think I'll just sit here for a while and relax." She jiggles the little silver bell.

"Sure. Well, tell Glo I hope she feels better." Then I practically trip over my chair, trying to get out of there.

At home, I find Mother and Aunt Dorothy stretched out on her king-size bed, playing gin rummy and watching *Hill Street Blues*. Merlie is right between them, looking all snug in her fluffy pink robe and matching slippers. "So?" says my mother, which means she's not mad at me and wants to hear all about my evening.

After I flop at the foot of the bed, I can't help muttering, "What a washout."

Aunt Dorothy perks up, curious as a hound dog aroused by a new scent. "What went on there, Roxie? You look perplexed."

"That's putting it mildly." Then I find myself giving a full description of Maggie Stern in her peekaboo robe, ending with a watered-down version of Glo bolting from the table.

At first, Aunt Dorothy starts laughing. But Mother shakes her head. "There is trouble."

"Maybe you're right," concedes Aunt Dorothy. "Trouble in paradise."

"Come on," I say. "This was just an off night." Then I can't help blurting, "Why would Mr. Stern tell Glo he thinks I look sloppy? I know he's a neatness freak, but . . ."

Aunt Dorothy clucks her tongue. "Some people are like that. Why, my dental hygienist told me that on her day off she goes to her son's school and helps clean the lunchroom. Teeth, dishes . . . whatever—she wants to rid the world of germs."

"No, that's not it," says Mother slowly. She and my aunt exchange looks.

"What is it, then?" I demand.

After a while, Aunt Dorothy says, "Roxie, let me tell you something. Mr. Stern has a narrow-minded attitude. You might say he's old-fashioned."

"He is a snob," Mother interjects.

"All right, then, here it is straight. If you don't come with the right credentials, look and act a certain way, you might as well be from Lower Slobovia, as far as he's concerned."

"What's he so uptight about? What's wrong with me?"

"You don't happen to fit the mold, that's all. Don't worry about it. His hands are so full trying to control his wife and daughters, he doesn't have time to bother about you."

"I wish—" Mother says, ". . . your father . . ." She sighs and looks away.

"Roxie *is* sloppy," pipes up Merlie.

With that, I pounce on her. "You've had it," I shout, piling the pillows over her squirrely little head. "There's just so much abuse one person can take!"

10

Saturday night Glo, Buffy, and I dress over at the Sterns'
for John's party. I've tried to put out of my mind that
awkward dinner the other night. Glo hadn't mentioned
it, so I haven't either. Getting dressed over here, I feel as
if I'm part of a magical inner circle again. I love the way
Maggie supervises the whole operation. If my mother saw
me now, she'd probably say, "You look awful," one of
her standard phrases.

"I can't wait," says Glo. "I feel as if something awe-
some is about to happen." What I'm experiencing is sheer
terror. Boys are not my best subject.

"Here, try on my sweater," orders Glo. It's a pink
Benetton with a low V in front.

"I feel ridiculous," I say, observing my reflection in the
mirror. "This pleated skirt doesn't exactly match." I
quickly pull off the sweater and change into my loose
Oxford shirt. Buffy is stuffed into snug Guess jeans and
an even tighter top. Tottering around on Irene's silver
heels, Glo zips up her denim jumpsuit. An unlikely com-

bination if ever I saw one! We've just sprayed pink patches into our hair and applied Jazzy Magenta to our lips. Lined in front of Maggie's full-length mirror, Buffy and Glo strike seductive poses. I slump in the middle and stick out my tongue. "Do that at the party," says Glo. "You're sure to be a hit."

"I look like a fat wad," wails Buffy. "I bet my real mother was an elephant."

Maggie's propped in bed, observing our efforts. "Glo darling, try brushing your hair back on one side." Glo pulls her wavy hair behind one ear. "Now, isn't that better?" Glo nods. "You all look spectacular," Maggie finally concludes after a few more gentle suggestions. "I wish I were going with you. Ray, come in and take a look at these girls. Aren't they fabulous?" Mr. Stern's in his sitting room studying *The Wall Street Journal* as if he's memorizing it. He's wearing a monogrammed silk robe, sapphire-colored to match his eyes. His blond hair is tousled over his forehead. Robert Redford, I used to think. Now he reminds me of one of those decadent aristocrats in a foreign film.

"Well, now," he comments, after instructing us to turn around a few times. "You girls are quite a sight." My sentiments exactly. "Does Irene know you're wearing her clothes?"

"No," says Glo, "but she always borrows everything of mine without asking."

"Two wrongs don't make a right," he replies.

"You always take her side."

"Now, Punkin," he says. "Don't get offended. Why don't I drive you to the party? I'll go in and have a drink with Bobsie and Henry." He gives her a pat on the head.

"You don't have to come in," Glo says, shrugging his hand away.

"Don't be silly. With all those kids messing up their house, the Lessers will probably be relieved to have another adult around," Mr. Stern insists.

"This is the pits," Glo says, rolling her eyes.

"My parents are dropping by, too," Buffy says in a resigned voice.

I think it's terrific the way these parents know each other. I wish my mother were a part of their group.

"You'll be all right, won't you, sweetie?" says Mr. Stern to his wife.

Maggie starts to hum, an impassive look on her face as if she's already forgotten we're here.

"Are you sure you want Dad to leave you alone?" asks Glo.

Mrs. Stern yawns. "Pour me a nightcap before you go, Ray, and don't forget to turn on Julio." Sometimes Maggie acts so spacey, I wonder if she's on something.

"Girls, give me a minute while I change." Mr. Stern disappears into his dressing room. A minute turns into thirty. Finally he emerges, looking impeccable, as usual, in a houndstooth sport coat and gray corduroy pants.

I smell a familiar scent. Aramis cologne. For a moment, if I shut my eyes, I can almost feel my father's presence in the room, the heady aroma of his cologne bringing him back to me. Suddenly I miss him so much I'm aching inside. I want to open my eyes and find my father right here with his arms reaching toward me. But when I look up, Mr. Stern is regarding me coolly.

"Ready?" he asks. The ache in my chest tightens.

"We've been ready for hours," says Glo. "What are you all spiffed up about?"

"I have to look my best when I'm escorting three beautiful women," he says. I feel my cheeks burn.

When we pull up to a huge house that reminds me of a feudal fortress, Mr. Stern turns off the motor and observes the three of us huddled in the back seat. We don't budge. "Now, girls," he chuckles. "Are you having stage fright?"

"Very funny, Dad."

We pile out and, locking arms, shuffle toward the house. John's father answers the door. After he's kissed Buffy and Glo, he looks down at me. "Well, now, who's this young lady?"

"Henry, don't you know Roxie Baskowitz? She goes to Bannister, too. Roxie, this is Dr. Lesser," Mr. Stern says.

I stick out my hand. "Very nice to meet you." My voice sounds too loud. Dr. Lesser is very tall, with a long face and thick, gray hair. He stoops over to peer at me through horn-rimmed glasses. "Baskowitz," he says, firmly shaking my hand. "Is your mother's name Frances?"

"Yes, do you know my mother?" I ask, praying he doesn't, and if he does, that he won't start telling me in front of everyone how sorry he is.

"Indeed. Wonderful woman. She was Hawkins's patient over at St. Luke's a few years ago." Dr. Lesser addresses his remarks to Stern. "A real trooper, Roxie's mother. No one's ever forgotten her there. The nurses still talk about the beautiful lady who was so sick but never complained. Never, during all those months in the hospital. How is she doing?" Dr. Lesser asks, still holding my hand.

"Oh, fine." Am I supposed to take my hand away first?

"What an amazing woman. I think Hawkins was a little in love with her. Please give her my best."

"I will," I mumble. If she's so wonderful, why is it so hard to live with her? Or am I the horrible one?

11

Downstairs the boys are assembled around the TV, engrossed in *Saturday Night Live.* I note that John is a carbon copy of his dad, minus the gray hair. He ambles over and offers me a can of Pepsi. "My brother said he'd stash a keg in the laundry room, but my mother already confiscated it." I glance around. Glo and Buffy are in the corner fiddling with the records. But Glo keeps her eyes glued on Tony, who lounges on the couch, his feet propped on the coffee table. We're the only girls here. "Do you know if the rest of the girls are coming?" he asks. "The guys have been hanging around here since six."

"Don't worry," I say. "They'll show. That's all we've been talking about." Actually I'm exaggerating, but the way John's face relaxes tells me I've said the right thing.

"Listen, Roxie. I'm sorry about the mix-up. This is the first time Mom's let me have a party. And, well, she made out the list. Invited the kids she knows."

"And their parents," I interject, rolling my eyes. We both laugh. "I'm glad you set her straight."

"Me too," he says, and then looks away shyly. "Mom was afraid the whole class would show if she didn't send invitations. Once my brother had this open swimming party. She'd just planted a thousand pink petunias. The next morning, on top of the petunias were two hundred beer cans."

"You're kidding!" I could picture hundreds of kids converging all at once, trampling Mrs. Lesser's pink petunias to death.

"Guess who had to pick up the beer cans?"

"Where was your brother?"

"He left for Camp Nebagamon and stuck me with the mess."

"Well, you're just a good kid," I say, thumping him on the back. Most boys make me nervous, especially the ones at school, who look through me as if I'm invisible, but I feel comfortable around John.

"Have a pretzel," he says, popping one in my mouth.

"Hey, John," calls Harry Morgan, "throw me a beer." The boys guffaw.

"Have a Diet Coke instead," John says, tossing him a can.

When he wanders back to the TV, I check out the room. On a long table are big wooden bowls of popcorn and potato chips. There are posters of Marilyn Monroe tacked on the walls, as well as a bulletin board covered with snapshots of the Lesser boys' friends. All the lights are turned on, casting the room in a bright, flat glow.

Glo motions me over. "Isn't Tony adorable? Do you think he'll talk to me?"

"If he doesn't, he's a jerk," says the ever-faithful Buffy.

A chorus of shrieks and loud thuds announces the arrival of Lucy and Cissy, the Baldwin twins, and their sidekick, Tammy Green. Glo calls them the Clones. They're exactly the same height and wear matching pastel Esprit miniskirts and angora sweaters.

"Watch them flip their hair back in unison," Glo whispers. Tammy is clutching a small Kodak. "Say cheese," she squeals, lifting the camera and snapping a picture of the boys, who pop up at once as if strings are attached to their heads. Then they sink down, reverting to the tube, while the six of us regroup by the pretzels.

"What do we do now? This evening could turn into a crashing bore," says Tammy, with an affected lilt to her voice.

"It's time to mobilize our forces," says Glo.

Tammy thrusts her head toward us and whispers, "If anyone could break up this captive audience, it's Tony."

"Go over and sit on his lap," suggests Lucy. Cissy nods. Glo bristles.

"You're not the only one who likes him," Tammy says to Glo. "He and I talk on the phone every night."

"Well, I don't call boys," Glo retorts. "We'll just see who he'd rather talk to."

Frankly, I wouldn't mind if we stayed in our separate corners. When everyone starts coupling off, what will I do?

"Turn up the stereo," Glo instructs Buffy. "I'll make the first move." She ambles over to the couch and, without a moment's hesitation, squeezes in between Tony and Harry. Within two minutes, Tony has his arm draped casually around her shoulders. Tony's defection causes a chain reaction. Soon Harry and the rest lose interest in TV in favor of some tentative mingling. The lights flicker on and off until only the television screen is illuminated. Moving against a back wall, I squint at the TV through the darkness. A model swings her hair, trying to sell hair spray. Then John turns down the sound and finds his way back to me.

"Hi again. Looks like the party's livening up," I say, snapping my fingers to the music to make him think I'm into it.

"I don't know," says John. "I'm not much of a partyer."

I stop snapping. "Me either."

"This whole thing was Mother's idea. She says, and I quote, 'An organized social life keeps young people off the streets.'" This is delivered in a high falsetto, which makes me laugh.

"Well, you're definitely safe from drug pushers, sadists, rapists, and hookers in Ladue, Missouri."

"That's the trouble. My parents set boundaries for me. Don't go here; don't go there. They have an aversion to anything that's not safe or familiar. Even most of my father's patients are his old friends."

"So how do you cross those safe boundaries?" I ask. "Throw a party on Washington Avenue?" That's where the thugs hang out.

"No. But my cousin's a doctor downtown. She works in a public health clinic. Pushers, addicts, robbers, she sees them all. When I get out of med school, that's where I'm headed." He pauses. "Of course, I have to get into med school first. My math grades aren't so hot."

"You've come to the right person," I say, but then I feel embarrassed, as if I'm bragging or being too pushy. I find a more laid-back tone. "I didn't figure you for a crusader. You really want to devote your life to helping losers?"

"Yes. I do. What's wrong with that?"

"Nothing. It's just that . . ." I can't find the right words. It's as if some huge objection to John's plan is pushing at me from deep inside, and I'm not sure what it is. We've moved back in a corner now, away from the rest of the kids, who are clustered in the center, not dancing exactly, but lurching around to the music.

"It's just that what?" John says in a voice that makes me know he's not feeling defensive, just interested in what I have to say.

"I don't know. You ought to meet my mother. She was a do-gooder, too."

"Was?"

"Before she got sick." My voice has gotten so soft I can barely hear myself talk. "Sorry. I didn't mean to bring that up. I don't even know what I'm trying to say." Why do I always relate everything back to me and my dumb problems?

"This is supposed to be a conversation," John says. "You can bring up whatever you want." It's strange, the way a light conversation can suddenly turn heavy. Someone you never even took seriously, someone who always seemed nice but ordinary, turns out to be altogether different.

"You just surprised me, that's all," I say, trying to change the subject back to him.

"What about your mother? Why did you call her a do-gooder, as if that's bad?"

"She was a social worker. That's all."

"Do you want to follow in her footsteps?" The way he leans toward me, his big shaggy face close to mine, I'm reminded of an eager puppy.

"This is going to disappoint you, but what I really want is to live in a mansion, wear exotic clothes, and be waited on all day like Mrs. Stern."

"Are you serious?" He looks disillusioned, as if he thought I might have been a possible Florence Nightingale to his Dr. Dooley.

Then it hits me, what's been bothering me all along, why this whole conversation about noble causes gets to me. "Look, my mother devoted her life to helping people. She and my dad worked so hard they never had time to go out. Then, when they could finally afford to buy a house and travel, they got shot down. Both of them. I'm going to live it up before that happens to me."

"Listen, I'm really sorry about your parents. But I can't believe you're as cynical as that 'eat, drink, and be merry' business sounds."

"Well, maybe I am cynical. That's the way I feel." Then I picture myself in a gold-lamé dress, sweeping around a huge house, giving lawn parties right out of *The Great Gatsby*. In the midst of this fantasy, I happen to look over to where Glo and Tony are stretched out on the couch. He's practically on top of her and they're kissing as if no one else is in the room. Tammy must have been watching, too, because the next thing I know, flash-bulbs are popping and she's hopping up and down, squealing, "I got them. I got them."

Glo and Tony bolt up. Glo starts screeching, but before anyone can stop her, Tammy goes racing up the stairs. For a second, everyone freezes. Then Glo, Tony, Buffy, and I chase after her. Now in the entrance hall, Tammy is batting her eyelashes innocently at Dr. Lesser and Mr. Stern.

"Oh, yes," she says, "I'm an amateur photographer." This pronouncement stops us from tackling her and bashing in the camera. If we grab it and proceed to make a scene, Dr. Lesser will want to know why, and then Tammy will naturally tell him. So we're stuck. Mr. Stern turns to Glo. "You'd better go straighten up, and then we're going home. Things are getting out of hand." Glo turns pale and gags. Buffy and I drag her into the guest bathroom.

"Tammy will go straight to Fotomat and pass those pictures all over school," Glo wails, holding her stomach.

"You'll be famous," says Buffy.

"And really popular," I add, trying to calm her down by making light of the whole affair.

"You think this is funny," says Glo, "but my life's ruined."

I turn on the cold water and hand her a towel. "Wipe your face. Throwing a fit will only make things worse."

"My stomach hurts. I want to go home." Slumping down on the toilet, she blows her nose into the towel, hiccups, gags, then grabs the wastebasket and throws up.

"Oh, no," groans Buffy. "What do we do now?"

At that moment, there's a knock. In walks Mrs. Marks. She's one of those husky, athletic types, and is wearing a brown velour jogging suit and tan Adidas. I've seen her sprinting around the lane with their cocker spaniel.

"Hi, Mom," says Buffy, moving to block the wastebasket. But it only takes Mrs. Marks a second to spot Glo. "Glo, for heaven's sake. Are you ill?" Glo nods miserably. "Have you kids been drinking?" Mrs. Marks asks, folding her arms and observing us suspiciously.

"Definitely not, Mommy. Promise," says Buffy in a little-girl voice.

Glo sniffs loudly and thrusts back her shoulders. "We don't drink. I have a nervous stomach. That's all." She gives Mrs. Marks her intense stare.

"Do you think you're all right now?"

"Yes," says Glo firmly.

"Then you girls go on out of here," Mrs. Marks says calmly, "and I'll clean up." Glo gargles and spits into the sink. Then, head high, she marches back into the entrance hall. The rest of the guests are leaving. The Clones file out, smirking.

"Don't let those boys leave until every kernel of popcorn, every potato chip, every empty can in the house is pitched," Mr. Stern tells Dr. Lesser, who's at the door, looking bewildered. Glo groans under her breath, and the three of us trudge down the walk to the car.

12

Bright and early Sunday morning, Glo calls. I glance at my alarm clock: 7:00 A.M. "Why must you wake me at this ungodly hour?"

"Are you kidding? I've been up all night. I waited as long as I could. What am I going to do? When Tammy gets those pictures back, she'll pass them around school, and I won't be able to show my face."

"Aren't you being overly dramatic?" I say, yawning.

"The kids will think I'm fast, call me a tramp and a slut . . ."

"Don't forget 'harlot' and 'whore of Babylon,' " I add.

"What am I going to do?"

"The question is, what in heaven's name were you doing, flat on the couch with Tony? Couldn't you two have gone into the laundry room if you wanted to give way to your unbridled passions?"

"Well, I wasn't giving way to my passions," Glo says, sniffing. "I just wanted to show that twit Tammy that Tony likes *me*."

"Evidently she got the picture."

"Very funny. Ohhh," moans Glo, "this is worse than the pits. And Tony's so cool. I hope things aren't ruined for us."

"Why don't you discuss this with him? Let Tony do something about those pictures if he's so cool." This whole obsession she has with Tony infuriates me. Glo doesn't say anything. "Look, I'll come over later when I'm fully conscious, and we can figure something out. Okay?" Sundays Glo and I usually hang out anyway.

Another pause. "Well, actually, Tony's coming over later," she says.

"Oh." That does it. Not only am I going to have to listen to her go on and on about Tony, but now she's planning to spend all her spare time with him.

"I'll call you later and tell you everything," says Glo.

"Sure," I say.

After we hang up, I drag myself out of bed and into the bathroom.

"You are a jerk, Mr. Tough Tony Sansone," I snarl into the mirror, screwing up my face to indicate utter disdain. "Who do you think you are, swaggering and strutting about, making Glo all quivery? You've got some nerve," I say and shake my fist.

This new development is about to ruin our weekends together. I wouldn't choose some boy over her—never. I march around my bedroom a few times and drag a chair back to the mirror, straddle it backward and peer at my reflection. Is there something wrong with me, or what? I have other thoughts in my head besides boys.

I take a closer look. I'm as gangly as John Lesser, no

question about it. My neck is too long, my ears too big, my mouth is so wide I could be mistaken for a Muppet! So what! The boys in my class are a bunch of cretins. Anyway, if I try, I can be sophisticated. Watch this! Blowing on an imaginary cigarette, I flutter my eyelashes and thrust my shoulder forward. "Hey, baby." But instead of sophisticated, I look idiotic—doing a Harpo Marx imitation instead of a Greta Garbo.

A couple of months ago, I hid a package of Marlboros and some matches in the back of my closet, waiting for the right moment to try one. It's now or never. I root through a pile of shoes and pull out the package. The cigarettes are probably stale, but I wouldn't be able to tell the difference anyway. Back in the john, I manage to pull one out and light up. I suck the smoke through my teeth and blow it out. The smoke streams forth and disappears into the mirror. I try it a few more times, admiring my style. I've no idea whether I'm doing it right, but as far as I can tell, there's not much to this. Just suck in and blow out. I wonder if I'm supposed to swallow the smoke. It seems a lot of effort for nothing, especially at seven o'clock in the morning.

"Roxie," comes a voice behind me. I whip around, smoke pouring out of my mouth. Mother rushes toward me, a horrified look on her face, and grabs for the cigarette in my hand. "Let go of me," I say, struggling to loosen her grip. She's so mad the veins are standing out on her forehead. With her face close to mine, I can see the jagged edge of the long white scar on her neck and the slight drooping edge of her mouth. I let the cigarette go. She drops my wrist and takes a step back.

"I'm just trying a cigarette. You don't have to make a federal case out of it."

"I don't like this. You are awful." Her breathing is heavy. Is she going to cry? But I can't stop myself now.

"I'm not awful, and I can smoke any time I want." I wave the pack of Marlboros at her. The minute I do this, I know it's a mistake. She lunges for the cigarettes as I push the chair forward and hurdle away from her.

"I can't stand this." My mother's voice sounds high-pitched and frayed.

"I can't stand it either," I scream. "Go away and leave me alone."

"Oh, Roxie, why can't you be good?"

"Okay, here. I don't want them anyway." I fling the pack across the room. The cigarettes fly out like missiles and scatter on the floor. Mother stares at me, then down at the floor in disbelief. Her eyes fill with tears. I push past her into the hall, running down the back steps and out the kitchen door. Merlie's bike is turned over on the grass. I yank it up by the handlebars and jump on, pedaling as fast as I can down the driveway. I don't know where I'm headed, but I take a left, coasting down the hill. The wind blows in my direction and slows the progress of the bike. With the air cool on my face and on my bare legs, I can't hold back the feeling of relief at being out of the house, free of my mother and her accusing looks. But I also need to get away from her tears and the awful fact that I'm the one who finally made her break down and cry.

I pedal hard and concentrate on moving forward so I can block out what's happened behind me. Hickory Lane crosses the main road. Cars stream toward me from both directions. I wait for the red light, then pump hard to get across before it turns green again. The bike clatters over a branch in the street. The sun hides behind clouds, and the sky is pearl-gray. The street curves and winds back on itself. On either side are rows of apartment buildings that lead to a shopping mall, and beyond that, my old neighborhood. Two young mothers sit on the grass watching their children race back and forth. A little girl jumps rope in the driveway. "One banana, two banana, three banana, four," she cries, her pigtails bouncing, her skirt flying up. Ahead, joggers are running silently, plugged into their headsets. I'd rather listen to the street sounds and the wind and the children, their voices high and sweet, like birds calling in the trees.

At St. Michael's Church, I slow down and weave in and out of the people headed for Sunday services. Where am I headed? I can't stop at Walgreen's for a candy bar or at Velvet Freeze for an ice cream. It's too early, but as I swerve past the mall, I find myself turning the corner down my old block. By Aunt Dorothy's house, I climb off the bike. Maybe this is where I wanted to go all along. Her green Chevy is parked crookedly in front. She's home, probably still sleeping. I retrieve the key from under the mat, push open the screen and unlock the door. Aunt Dorothy hid the key there after the night when Mother got sick and Merlie had to bang on the window to wake her up. At that time, she wanted to break her lease and move in with us, but Mother talked her out of it.

Aunt Dorothy was married once a long time ago, but

I can't remember much about her husband, and she never talks about him. During the day, she's a trust officer at the Pony Express Bank, and at night, when she's not with Mother, she works on a novel that's supposed to be a family saga, mystery, and gothic romance—all in one. Inside the house, I can hear the clacking of her typewriter, which means she's up.

"Aunt Dorothy!" I shout, cutting through the living room to her study.

Her fingers are flying over the keys as if they're on automatic. Wads of crumpled paper lie strewn across the floor. When she turns and sees me at the doorway, she cocks her head in surprise. "Good heavens, Roxie, what are you doing here?"

"I was in the neighborhood, so I decided to visit."

"At this hour?" she asks, swiveling the chair to face me.

"How's the book going?" I ask.

"It's almost eight hundred pages, with no end in sight. At the moment, the heroine is hiding from her wicked uncle in a deserted cabin that's haunted by a ghost." She shakes her head. "I just can't decide how to get her out of this."

"How about being rescued by a handsome prince?"

"That's an original thought," she says, laughing. "But you didn't come all the way over here to discuss my literary progress. Clear away that pile of books and sit down." I settle into the armchair. "Did you have another fight with your mother?"

"How did you guess?"

"So what else is new? I don't have to be a genius to see what goes on between you two—at each other's throats all the time. Your mother was headstrong at your age, too. No one could ever tell her what to do. That's what makes things so difficult for her now." Aunt Dorothy bites her lower lip and frowns. "She was always so independent, so confident at everything. Even your dad couldn't stop her if she had her mind set on something. She was determined to earn her Master's, have a career, and take care of two little girls at the same time. She managed beautifully, too. Then it all fell apart." Aunt Dorothy stares out the window. "Your mother had been standing on a pedestal, the world at her feet. Then she toppled off."

"She didn't stay home and take care of us," I say. "You go on about her as if she were some kind of saint. Listen, I know how she used to be." Every day of my life I think about it, wishing we could go back. "But I have to put up with her now, always criticizing me, never pleased with anything I do."

"She's worse on herself." Aunt Dorothy sighs. "You just don't realize it."

" 'You are awful. It's not right.' That's all Mother can say to me."

"Roxie, don't you understand that every time she speaks, it comes out exaggerated and sounds worse than normal because she can't express herself any other way?"

"She hates my hair. She hates the way I act, the way I look. She drives me nuts," I say, pacing back and forth across the room. "Glo's mother always praises her."

"I'm sure Glo's mother criticizes her, too, but she might be more subtle about it. Your mother can't do it that way. She simply can't talk any better. Imagine how frustrating it is for her." Aunt Dorothy gets up and stretches. "Oh, Roxie, I don't need to tell you how it is. You two have to work things out."

"I know we do. But I haven't figured out how." Together, we pick up the scattered papers and stuff them in the wastebasket.

"Try putting yourself in her place sometime," my aunt says.

"How can she take it?" I ask softly. "I'd kill myself." I've tried to imagine not being able to talk. It scares me to think about it. Sometimes, after Mother and I fight, I'm afraid she will kill herself, and then it would be my fault.

Aunt Dorothy stands by my side, touching my shoulder. I look into her eyes, and I know she understands. "I've thought that a hundred times, Roxie. When your father died, I didn't know how she'd take it. But at the funeral she said to me in that way she has of saying things —short and absolutely to the point: 'The children, they have to grow up.' She's a practical person, your mother, and she's tough, very tough." Aunt Dorothy pulls me close and puts her arm around me. "Your father used to say, 'Promise you'll take care of Franny if anything ever happens to me.' But sometimes I think it's the other way around. When Dave and I were divorced, she bought me this typewriter and told me to write everything down. When I get lonely, Franny listens to me. How can I feel sorry for myself when I look at her? She's never let up, not for a minute." Maybe that's what upsets me, I think. My mother never lets up—not on herself or on me.

"Come downstairs and have a piece of fruit. Unless you want some scrambled eggs." I shake my head no. "I'm on a diet myself," she says, sucking in her stomach.

Aunt Dorothy's forever on a diet, but she never looks any different.

"If you exercised," I tell her, "you could eat whatever you wanted." In the kitchen, she turns on the light and points to the bowl of apples on the table as if they contained cyanide. "The minute I wake up, I feel like eating something gooey. There's no way I can pretend an apple is a piece of cake. Now, what's all this about *me* exercising?"

"I'm teaching a class at school for the little kids. It's a combination of jazz and aerobics. I think you ought to try something like that."

"Sounds interesting," she says, handing me a bag of Oreos.

"Mother's not too impressed." Suddenly, I'm starving. I sit opposite my aunt. We munch on the cookies, handing the bag back and forth.

"Maybe she just doesn't understand what your job is about," says Aunt Dorothy. "Franny's not very loose with praise. She has to see what you're doing, I think, before she can get excited about it."

"She hasn't been to my school once since I started going there. The other mothers always come for meetings."

"I think she's a little self-conscious around those other mothers. It's hard for her. Maybe I'll come by school with her one day, or Herman can. I'm sure he'd love it." I scrunch my face. "Now, what's wrong with Herman?"

"What's wrong with Herman? He's a total loser, that's what's wrong with him."

Aunt Dorothy wrinkles her nose. "That's not fair. He's a nice person." She says this as if she's chosen each word carefully. I can tell my aunt's not quite sure about it either. "I just don't want Franny to get hurt."

"I don't see you going out on dates," I say, curling my lip.

"Well, now, aren't you being a bit judgmental? Frankly, I've never had much luck with men. Now I guess I'm used to being alone. But that doesn't mean your mother is, and you can't expect that from her anyway. You'll see, one of these days you'll start to notice the boys, and you'll understand what I'm trying to tell you."

"Hah." And I pop a cookie in my mouth, letting the icing melt under my tongue.

The phone rings. The way Aunt Dorothy looks over at me, I know it's Mother, probably having a fit about me. "She's over here, Franny. She'll be home soon." Replacing the receiver on the hook, my aunt regards me. "One of these days, Roxie, some nice boy is going to come around, and then you won't be so contemptuous of love." She prances over and tweaks me on the cheek.

"Cut it out!" I shout. But I can't help laughing.

Later that night in bed, I close my eyes and think about what Aunt Dorothy said about my mother, how stubborn she is and how much alike we are in that way. Mother has such hard-and-fast rules about how things should be done. I thought she'd changed because she got sick, but maybe she's always been that way, which means she's never going to be any different.

13

Monday morning comes too soon, and I feel overburdened by absolutely everything. How can I get out of bed and go to school? All I want to do is hide here under the covers. Mrs. Stern has the right idea, spacing out with the predictable music of Julio Iglesias and the movements of the sun. What a traumatic weekend. Mother's barely speaking to me, and Glo dumped me for Tony on Sunday. She'll probably stick with him at school, and I'll feel like a third wheel. The alarm keeps beeping, proclaiming the beginning of another week that's supposed to be the first day of the best week of my life. My motivation level is at an absolute zero.

I drag myself out of bed and into the bathroom. I look into the mirror. Dark eyes, lips that pucker. My father used to call my face "that silly mug of the moon." Peering at myself, I vow to stay out of the Tony/Glo affair. If she wants to be with him instead of with me, that's up to her. As for those dumb pictures, I don't want to be involved. Considering the state of the world, it's all much ado about nothing.

At breakfast, I try to make amends. I tell my mother what Dr. Lesser said about her. She looks pleased. I ask Merlie if she wants to sit with me on the bus. Merlie declines, knitting her eyebrows. "What's the matter? Don't you have anyone else to sit with?" she asks.

Instead of going to the corner to wait for the bus with Buffy and Glo, I stay with Merlie in front of our house. But the minute I get on, I can see there's trouble. Glo's wearing a desperate look on her face as she motions me over.

"What's happening?" I ask. Still peeved about Sunday, I keep my face stiff.

"They've got the pictures," she says. The boys are snickering as they pass Glo and Tony's photograph around. The general mood is one of hilarity—that is, until Tony gets on. Quickly, Harry sticks the picture into his notebook.

"What are you guys staring at me for?" Tony asks menacingly.

"Wouldn't you like to know," hoots Tammy.

"If it's that dumb picture, you'd better hand it over before I punch in your face," says Tony. He grabs Harry's books and dumps them on the floor. Four people scramble to retrieve the picture. I find myself down there, too, bumping heads, pushing and shoving, until the driver pulls over to the side of the road and presses hard on the brakes. I fall backwards into John's lap, feeling the sharp folds of his jacket, and his arms tighten around me. We sprawl there for a moment, then hoist ourselves up.

"In your seats, on the double," shouts the driver, "before I have a nervous breakdown." Why do they always hire bus drivers who hate kids or have mental problems?

"Goodbye, Romeo and Juliet," says John, shredding the picture and sprinkling the pieces out the window.

"I have another one," yells Tammy.

"Keep it as a souvenir," Tony says. "You can see what you're missing." He winks at Glo, whose face lights up with relief and pride. This is the moment in one of those old melodramas when the heroine, after being rescued by the handsome stranger, sighs and says, "My hero," rolling her eyes in ecstasy. Makes me want to barf! We scoot back to our seats, the bus lurches forward, and the rest of the ride to school is relatively peaceful.

In social studies we're learning about the Declaration of Independence from a slide show that flashes the text, along with photographs of Mrs. Wooster's trip to Washington, D.C. "We hold these truths to be self evident." Then a picture of Mrs. Wooster and her husband waving in front of the Lincoln Memorial. "That all men are created equal." Mrs. Wooster again, posing on the steps of the White House. This goes on until we reach "Under God, with liberty and justice for all." Mrs. Wooster turns on a tape of the National Anthem and signals us to stand. Singing along, we focus on the last picture, a large close-up of the Woosters and our congressman shaking hands in front of the American flag.

"Is this supposed to prepare us for college?" whispers John behind me.

At "The rocket's red glare, the bombs bursting in air," I realize that today's not just an ordinary Monday. Today's the day I'm supposed to meet Aerobics Eddie during lunch hour. The entire class blasts out the last line at the top of their lungs: "The land of the free, the home of the brave."

"Very good," Mrs. Wooster says, beaming, as if we're a bunch of third graders.

When the bell finally rings, I race to the gym. Eddie's there waiting in shiny purple tights, blue Bannister gym shorts, and a T-shirt. He's tucked his records under his arm. "Hi, doll," he says. "Change your clothes and we'll roll." The Primary School is across the green in the former house of the first headmaster of Bannister. It's a red brick colonial with green shutters and a slate roof, surrounded by a white picket fence to keep the kids from wandering off. The garage has been converted into a mini-gym.

The children are clustered on the floor of the gym, rolling into each other like round, bright marbles. When the teacher claps, they freeze. Fifteen pairs of eyes are directed at Eddie, who bounds into the center of the room. "Kids, I know your teachers have given you a speech about being good and keeping quiet, but as far as I'm concerned, you can make as much noise as you want. I only have two rules. Move your bodies when I move mine, and laugh at my jokes." The children elbow each other and giggle. They look totally out of control—little bundles of dynamite.

"Roxie," calls Eddie. "Come over here." Cautiously, I enter the circle. "This is my assistant and the best student I have in the Upper School." I inch toward the door. The children eye me suspiciously. "Upsy-daisy, my little cabbages," says Eddie. "Follow me." He wiggles his body. "We're jellyfish. Let's shake it up." One by one, the children begin to mimic him, their bodies uncurling, bending, and twirling to the music. "We're stepping on a bed of nails. Lift those feet. We're windmills. Wave your arms." Before I know it, we're all swaying back and forth, being windmills with Eddie. If a stranger happened to drop in, he would see a room full of happy, shrieking children, hurling themselves around the room. But I can tell the children are trying to follow, even if their timing and coordination are off.

Only one kid holds back. Scrawny, with wide, solemn eyes, he slouches in the corner, ripping the Velcro strap on his sneakers. He pulls it off and on to the beat of the drums. It's not as if he's acting up or causing trouble, but something about his attitude catches my attention, draws me over.

"Hi." I squat down to be on his level. "It's easy. Anyone can do it." He doesn't answer, but he's looking hard at me. "Do you want to dance?" I ask.

"I don't know how." His voice sounds mushy, as if he's swallowing his words.

"What's your name?"

"Jimmy," he mumbles.

I hold out my hand. "Okay, Jimmy, if you want, I'll dance with you." He backs away. Even on my knees, I must seem big to him.

I remember once in nursery school when a big teacher positioned herself over me during rest hour. "I can see you blinking," she rasped in my ear. "You're not sleeping. Don't try to fool me." I squeezed my eyelids shut and refused to stir. But I was scared all the same. Maybe Jimmy's scared, too.

I sit cross-legged and flex my muscle. "Do you know why this is called a muscle?" I ask him. Jimmy shakes his head no. "Because a long time ago, when they were inventing words, a Roman soldier flexed his muscle and thought the ripple looked like a little mouse running up and down his arm. The Latin word for mouse is *musculus.*"

"Jumping jacks!" shouts Eddie. "In a circle, watch Roxie."

"Duty calls," I tell Jimmy. "Maybe next time." He shrugs, but I can see the corner of his mouth turn up into a faint smile when I flex my muscle again.

While Eddie watches from the bench, wiping his forehead with a towel, I attempt to lead the group. "Hey, you guys. Call me Roxie. Now, what's my name?"

"Roxie," chime a few voices.

"What? I can't hear you!"

"Roxie!" they all shout.

"That's better. Now, let's go!"

Mass confusion results—tangled arms, legs, bobbing heads, and me in the center. After twenty jumping jacks, I'm not even out of breath, but the kids are losing momentum.

"Three minutes left," signals Eddie. Uh-ho, I think, what am I going to do now? They're all lined up like baby ducks, waiting for my next move. Then it hits me.

"For my last number, ladies and gentlemen, we're going to play follow-the-leader." The kids prance, sometimes skipping or hopping behind me as we form a long snake, curling from one side to the other. When I pass my little friend in the corner, I pause for a moment and whisper, "Want to be leader with me?" This time, when I reach out, he grabs my hand. As we weave around the room, I raise him high in the air. He lands lightly and bounces up again as if he were on springs. One-two-three up, one-two-three up. The beat goes faster and faster. We are practically flying.

"Wheee," he sings, lifting his arms high above his head. When the music stops, the children crowd around us, shrieking, "Do that to me, do that to me!" "Jimmy, you're so lucky!" He's smiling now, a wide grin that takes over his face. I feel his excitement, and my own, because I've thought of something to bring him in and it worked for both of us. Small bodies press against me, squealing and tugging. Then another idea strikes me, and I find myself calling out over the noise, "Everyone take a partner. We'll show you another fun thing to do." First, Jimmy and I demonstrate, his back to me, our arms clasped above our heads. Then, two by two, the children copy us. Finally, with the last note of the song, fifteen worn-out ragamuffins tumble to the ground.

Eddie pats me on the back. "Terrific! They loved it."

"They'll be lambs for the rest of the day," says Mrs. Weir, the Primary School teacher. She pulls me aside. "I haven't seen Jimmy this enthusiastic for weeks. It's practically impossible to get him to participate in anything."

"Why does he seem so sad?"

"His father died several months ago. He's still extremely upset."

"I can understand that." I see him eyeing us, his face wary, as if he knows we're talking about him.

"I'll be back next week," I tell Mrs. Weir. Then I wave and smile at Jimmy. He raises his arm and makes a little muscle.

"Let's get crackin', Superwoman," says Eddie.

"I could leap across the school yard in a single bound. That was really fun."

"You handled yourself like a professional. I couldn't have done better."

By this time, we're at the back door of the Upper School. The bell rings, and kids pour out, on their way to soccer practice. To keep from being trampled, Eddie and I move back against the holly bushes. Glo and Tony walk by, holding hands. They don't even notice me. I take a deep breath. My high from the class is beginning to level off. Now I'm faced with the same old dilemma.

"What's wrong?" asks Eddie. "Your shoulders are sagging, as if you're carrying the weight of the world."

"It's just that everything's changing. My mother's going out on dates. My friend Glo's falling in love. And I don't know what I want."

"Things change all the time. Life wouldn't be very interesting if they didn't. You're changing, too, even if you don't realize it. You can't stop the clock or turn it back. Don't even try. Roll with the punches."

"I guess you're right. But sometimes I feel so grown up and other times like a baby."

"That's what's great about being fifteen," he says. "You can act any way you want. If I behaved that way, they'd pronounce me certifiably insane."

"They already have," I said, "but I think I'll take your advice."

14

After the last bell, I stuff my books in my knapsack and take off down the hall. Glo and Tony are practically nose to nose on the front steps. Glo leans against the white column, and I can tell by the way her head is cocked that Tony's getting the full treatment: eye contact, dazzling smile. As I hurry past them, I give her a feeble wave and raise my eyebrows a couple of times.

"Hold on, Roxie," she calls. "I've been waiting for you." Glo skips toward me, two steps at a time. With her hair flying, her face lit up, she reminds me of a fairy sprite, the kind who's supposed to live under a toadstool in nursery stories. "Did you see us?" she mouths.

"How could I help it? With that ear-to-ear grin, you looked like an ad for a toothpaste commercial." I head quickly for the bus before she can start quizzing me. But before I know it, she's climbing on, sliding in next to me, still grinning idiotically. "I think I'm in love," she moans.

I choose to ignore the remark, and ask, "Where's good old Charlie today?"

"Who knows? I haven't seen our car, and I don't feel like waiting around for him." She pokes me when Tony gets on. He's so busy trying to act cool, he almost trips over her foot.

"When's the wedding? I think he might like you," I whisper.

She shakes her head and frowns.

"The pornography problem is solved. What's wrong now?" I ask.

She scoots down in the seat and hugs her stomach. "I feel queasy right here."

"Again? Have you talked to your mother about it? Maybe you should go to the doctor's." At the least sign of a runny nose, Mother drags me or Merlie to ours. I think she's afraid some rare infection will creep up and take us by surprise, the way the bubble burst in her brain.

"I don't want to bother Maggie," says Glo. "Besides, my dad will just say I'm high-strung."

"Well, you ought to find out what's wrong."

Glo leans closer. "You should have seen Irene today. She practically made a scene in the cafeteria, she was so furious. That other picture of me and Tony was passed around her class. She said I *mortified* her!"

"Well, maybe it was worth it just for that." We laugh.

"By the way, where were you during lunch hour? I've never known you to pass up yellow rolls and roast beef."

"I was teaching with Aerobics Eddie at the Primary School," I say casually.

"You and Aerobics Eddie?" she asks in a teasing voice. That's when I decide not to say anymore. I don't want her to make fun of this job. "John Lesser might get jealous."

"What are you talking about?"

"That's what Tony and I were discussing on the steps. He and John have this plan for Friday night. They want to come over. Spring break's coming, and then I go to Sarasota. Let's have some fun before I leave."

I press my nose against the window, watching cars, houses, and trees fly by. I picture gangly John Lesser peering down his long nose at me. "Well, at least he's taller than I am, and his father's a nice man, as my mother would say. But don't you think we have fun by ourselves?"

Her big blue eyes widen. "Sometimes I worry about you."

"But what if you and Tony go off nibbling in a corner somewhere? What do I do with John?"

"You can resort to good old-fashioned conversation, or you can turn on the tube."

"We have more fun together without boys." But I know I'm fighting a losing battle. After all, for years I watched my mother and my aunt sitting around together night after night doing nothing. Mother's much happier going out. And then I think of the Princess sweeping off with Sheldon Shapiro while Glo and I stayed home with rented rock videos. Maybe it is time to get out of our rut and try a new form of entertainment.

I shift my head to take a peek at John Lesser, who's sprawled out on the back seat of the bus, with a baseball cap pulled down over his face. His sneakers are untied, and his shirttail hangs out of his Levi's. In that position, he's hardly the type to make a girl's head spin, especially mine. In fact, I have a feeling the opposite sex is probably the last thing he has on his mind.

"Oh, now I get it," I say, turning to Glo. "You and Tony cooked up this whole scheme just so you two could be together. John didn't request the pleasure of my company, did he?" How could Glo think that I wouldn't catch on to their little plan?

She shrugs. "My dad says I can't go out with Tony but he can come over as long as we're not by ourselves."

"Good. Ask *him* to keep John company."

"You'd better make up your mind or I'll have to ask Buffy. I'm desperate. How am I ever going to start my education in sex and seduction, or live up to my wild and woolly reputation, if you don't help?"

"Give me a few minutes to ruminate in silence," I say, squeezing my eyelids shut. I press my fists to my forehead and begin breathing in low gasps.

"You're a lunatic," says Glo.

"Quiet. I'm thinking deep and dirty thoughts." In reality, my thoughts are pretty tame—especially when it comes to John Lesser. He's not exactly a wimp, but I wouldn't know what to do if I were left alone with him. When Glo describes the quiver she gets when she's around Tony, I don't even know what she's talking about. I love the idea of romance in books or in the movies, but all this monkey business in real life confuses me to no end. First, I have to deal with my mother going out, and now Glo's acting goofy.

By this time, the bus has reached her house. She casts a meaningful glance in my direction. "We'll see," I say, unwilling to give in but not wanting to start a feud either. "You'd better do it" is the only way to interpret the look thrown my way as she flounces off the bus. Something warns me no good can come of this.

A moment later, I'm home. There's an unfamiliar car in the driveway, an old-fashioned job with a huge grille and long, curved silver fenders. Inside the house, I find my mother seated on the living-room couch, pouring coffee. Next to her is a strange man. If I were asked to describe him in one word, I might say "gray." What's left of his hair is gray; he's wearing a gray pin-striped suit with a grayish-blue tie, and he has no distinguishing features. A totally nondescript person.

"You must be Rochelle. I'm Herman Levin." He stands and thumps my hand as if he's overjoyed to meet me.

"Roxie," I say. "I don't like to be called Rochelle."

"I don't blame you. It sounds more like a suburb in New York than a young lady's name." He lets out a honking laugh. My mother smiles. I grimace. He takes a step back. "Your mother and I are having a little chat. Would you like to join us?"

"Sure," I say, feeling trapped. We both sit and give each other the once-over. He seems harmless enough. What do they have to chat about? My mother doesn't chat, anyway. "Is that your car?" I say, pointing out the window.

"It's an old Daimler. I used to be in the car business." Oh, no, I think, a used-car salesman.

"So, where did you meet my mother?" I ask him, not only because I've been brought up to make polite conversation, but because I'm curious.

"Franny and I went to Soldan High together. In those days, it was the best public school in town. I think half our graduating class became lawyers or doctors, and the rest went into business. Now Soldan's smack in the middle of the ghetto. The old neighborhood is a blighted area." He pauses before he continues his stroll down memory lane. "But your mother was something in those days. Franny wasn't interested in being a pom-pom girl or the prom queen, although she could have had the crown in a minute. Am I right, Franny?"

"Well, I don't know," says my mother slowly.

"No, Franny was more interested in running the school. I'll never forget the editorial in the *Soldan Diary.*" Mother smiles. "You were upset that the teachers made such a big production out of Christmas, decorating the whole school with tinsel and colored lights. Remember those little fir trees in every classroom? But nothing for Hanukkah." He leans toward me, shaking his finger. "And sixty percent of the school was Jewish. Now, what was that last line?" He wrinkles his brow. "Oh, yes: 'Let's deck the halls for Hanukkah and light eight candles for peace.' " He leans back and pats my mother's arm. "That was at the height of the cold war. Some of our boys were being called overseas for the Berlin crisis. And of course, a few years later there was the war in Vietnam."

Even though Herman's not the greatest storyteller, I like hearing him talk, picturing my mother in another time, another place, before she got sick. "So, what happened?"

"We did it. We lit the—" She wants to say menorah. I can tell by the way she's shaking her head that she can't find the word. "What is it?" she asks herself.

"Menorah, Franny," prompts Herman in a kind voice. "I know," Mother says. "Oh, it is awful."

He squeezes her arm and pours himself another cup of coffee. "More for you, Franny?" Mother shakes her head and sets her cup on the coffee table.

"So," she says to me. "How was school?"

"It was all right." Herman smiles at me, relaxing on our couch as if he owns it. Since we're sitting here chatting, I might as well find out what his story is. Only four o'clock. Most people are still at work. "So, what do you do now?"

"I owned a chain of stores in Des Moines. We sold automobile parts. Sold it last year after my wife died." He looks over at Mother and shrugs. "I'm opening a new store here to be near my daughter and her husband."

"Motherrr," calls Merlie from upstairs. "I can't find any tennis balls. Do you know where they are?" All Merlie thinks about is tennis. Her biggest decision is which tennis dress to wear. I don't remember my life ever being that uncomplicated.

My mother smooths her skirt. "I will come back. You and Herman talk." I sniff and stare at the end table. Neither of us seems to have anything to say.

"I've been pretty lonely without my wife," he finally begins. "I'm sure Franny's been lonely, too. Does your mother have much company?" Now, why did he have to ask such a dumb question? What am I supposed to say? No, my mother never dates, and I like it that way. Or is he fishing for information?

"She has company," I mumble.

"Well, I'm very glad to renew an old acquaintance. I don't know very many people in St. Louis anymore. She seems happy to see me again," Herman says in a firm tone. I see that, like it or not, he's determined to stick around.

15

At dinner, Merlie, Mother, and I arrange ourselves around the table. Our first course always consists of grapefruit, followed by green salad and then either baked, broiled, or fried chicken. They say that chicken ranks as America's number-one favorite food. My mother has definitely contributed to the national average. Tonight's feast is chicken à la Shake 'n Bake. By the time I grow up, I figure I will have consumed at least three thousand chicken breasts. I hope I marry someone who hates chicken.

"Herman's nice," says my mother. She looks around, waiting for a response.

"He's all right," I say. "Is he an old boyfriend?"

Mother nods. "He was always a nice boy."

"He's not a boy, Mother, he's a man." It annoys me when she repeats herself, even though I know she can't help it. "Can you tell us more about him?" I ask, trying to be more patient, hating myself for causing another hurt look.

"He's . . . " Mother begins, then pauses, unable to go on, to find the word she needs. "Well, my mother liked him. He would . . . " She grabs Merlie's hand and shakes it. "He did that every time."

"You mean he had good manners?" Merlie says. "What about Daddy? Did your mother like him?"

Mother nods. "Daddy . . . he was . . . nice, too." She gives us that "Oh, well" gesture with her hand and looks away. I know her mind is filled with memories she wants to share but can't. I feel the pressure building in my head, making me want to shout out, "Try, just try for once to tell us," but I know she's unable to find the words, no matter how hard she tries.

We don't discuss much of anything except what Merlie or I did at school, basic stuff like that. But I'm not in the mood to describe what went on today. Except for teaching at the Primary School, the day was a complete bust. Like Glo, my mother doesn't take my class with Aerobics Eddie seriously, though. I push peas around on my plate and fall into a deeper funk.

Merlie chatters away, totally oblivious. "And then I missed the ball, right in the middle of set point, and fell down." She sticks her leg up. "See, I skinned my knee."

Mother makes a wry face. "Awful."

Merlie's eyes fill with tears. "It *was* awful. The other team laughed." Looking at her little white leg all covered with bruises, I remember the time when I fell off a jungle gym in nursery school and cut my lip open. They reached Dad, who rushed from the office to get me. He swept me into his arms and carried me to his car. I hid my head against his chest so no one could see me cry. He didn't tell me to act brave or stop being a crybaby. He didn't even mind that there was blood all over his shirt. He just kissed away my tears and told me he loved me. Merlie didn't have Dad around as long as I did and doesn't seem to remember things like that. It makes me feel sad that Mother can't fill in details for her or share old stories with us. Sometimes I think if we could talk about Dad it would keep me from missing him so much.

When the phone rings, I leap from my chair to answer it, but Merlie gets there first. She puts her hand over the receiver and in an abnormally loud whisper says, "Roxie, it's a boy!"

I grab the phone and shake my fist at her. "Hello."

The voice on the other end sounds a bit wobbly. "Roxie, this is John. You know, John Lesser."

"Yeah," I say. "I know."

"Oh, Roxie," Mother sighs. "Don't say yeah."

"Look, I have to change phones," I say to John. "Hold on a minute." To Merlie I hiss, "Hang this up the minute I pick up the other phone." She sticks her tongue out. Naturally, Mother misses it.

I practically trip going up the stairs, and my heart is thumping. "So what's happening?" I say into the mouthpiece. I sit stiffly on the edge of my bed, clutching the phone.

"Nothing much," says John. "Did you have fun at my party the other night?"

"It was okay." I can't work up much enthusiasm. "Did Glo tell you to call me?"

Silence. After a moment, he says, "It's Tony and Glo, the Dynamic Duo. They have this idea that we go over to her house Friday night, you know, the four of us together." The words come out rushed as if he's memorized them and is afraid he'll forget.

"I don't know. Sounds like a dumb idea to me."

"I absolutely agree with you. But she says her father won't let Tony come there alone." He sounds more relaxed now.

"You mean we're elected as chaperones?"

He laughs. "Something like that."

"What do you think?" I say, stretching out.

"Well, it's not like a party or anything. I mean, what are we supposed to do all night?"

"Glo and I generally drive Irene crazy or watch television."

"Irene's got a date with my brother. It's one big family affair."

"Well, we can drive your brother crazy, too." It's easy to talk to John. At least we're both stuck in the same predicament.

"Tony's called six times already, and my mother's threatened to pull the plug. If you don't go, Glo says Buffy Marks will. Then I'll have to sit around all night and talk about cocker spaniels."

"Maybe I could join you," I suggest. "A fivesome."

"The operative word is foursome."

"I'll think about it."

"Don't think about it. Just say yes, so I can get them off my back. Bring your books. Remember you offered to help me with math?"

"How about doing crossword puzzles? Or we can read to each other out loud, maybe from the Old Testament."

We both laugh. "All right, I give in." John's actually nice, even if he does look like an overgrown rabbit.

"Great! See you tomorrow." Before I even have a chance to say goodbye, he hangs up.

Two minutes later, the phone rings. I pick it up. "Hi, Glo."

"How did you know?"

"I have these extrasensory vibes. I told John yes. So don't bug me anymore."

"I knew you'd come through. I promise to do anything you want for a week."

"Only a week? I think this is worth at least a year's commitment."

"Guess what?" she whispers, her voice full of mischief. "Dad's actually going away on business. And you know Maggie, she'll be out like a light by eight o'clock."

"It's not that I want to lead a dreary life. In fact, I'm ready for adventure. But I was thinking in terms of Tom Sawyer and Huckleberry Finn, not the Dating Game."

"Well, you have to start somewhere. Cheer up. We're on the threshold of a new era," Glo says dramatically.

"That's what I'm afraid of."

16

Friday night, while Mother waits for Herman to pick her up, she primps in the hall mirror. She's wearing a new silk dress, black, with huge red poppies. I've never seen her in such a flamboyant outfit, which confirms my worst suspicions. This afternoon she put away the paint buckets and rolled up the plastic. But she didn't finish painting. I can still see the globs of dry enamel where I botched the job.

I station myself by the front door. I want to be on hand when the doorbell rings, to watch for any signs of lust, which has reached epidemic proportions in our neighborhood. But maybe it's not as bad as I think. "Renew an old acquaintance." That's what Herman said. Mother's just being polite, dressing up and putting out a snack, even if it is that fancy French cheese, the kind that smells gross and runs all over the plate. But she's already opening the door before he even knocks, gesturing him in, smiling as if she's been waiting all day just for this moment. He hands her a bottle of wine.

"How nice," my mother says in a proper voice.

"Let's sit and have a drink first," Herman suggests. "We've plenty of time before the concert." He actually takes her elbow, escorts her in, and pulls out a chair. Mother starts to uncork the bottle, but she can't manage with her weak hand.

Herman doesn't act as if he notices the crumbly cork. He simply takes the bottle and removes what's left of the cork and fills their glasses. "To the class of '55," he says, raising his goblet. They laugh.

The doorbell rings. "I'll get it," I say. John Lesser, with his T-shirt hanging out and a baseball cap worn backward, thrusts a game of Trivial Pursuit in my hands.

"What do you think?" he asks, without saying hello.

"Glo hates board games, but it's worth a try."

"Tony loves them. He's got an amazing memory. He can even recite lines from *Hamlet.*"

"Glo thinks Shakespeare's an American Indian. They make a perfect couple. So, what are you doing here?"

"I thought we could walk over to Glo's together, maybe plan a little strategy in case the Dynamic Duo duck out on us. I figure the only way to keep them from wandering off by themselves is to tie them up."

I look him up and down. "Nice of you to dress for the occasion."

"Huh?" He raises his eyebrows.

"Never mind." Now I don't have to bother changing my sweat clothes, which I always throw on after school because they're soft and comfortable. Sometimes I even sleep in them.

"Who is it?" my mother calls out from the other room.

"Come in to meet my mother," I say reluctantly. "She's in the dining room having cheese and wine."

"Cheese and wine?" repeats John.

"That's some kind of ritual older people go through before they go out on dates."

He gives me an odd look. Mother's sitting there chewing on a cracker, a blob of Brie sticking to her lip. I clench my fist. How can I introduce my mother to John with cheese on her face? Then I remember my Aunt Dorothy's signal. I've seen her scratch her nose when we're out to dinner, to let Mother know. As I start frantically to scratch, Herman takes his napkin, reaches up, and gently brushes the crumbs off. Without skipping a beat, he stands up. "How do you do, young man, I'm Herman Levin. This is Roxie's mother, Mrs. Baskowitz." I nod at him gratefully.

John offers his hand. "John Lesser, sir. My father wanted me to tell you hello, Mrs. Baskowitz."

"Thank you," my mother says. To my relief, she doesn't try to say any more.

At this point, John is leaning against the edge of the table, with his long legs crossed in front of him. As he starts to uncurl himself and straighten up, his feet scoot out from under him and he falls back against the table. There's a crunching noise, and the glass top cracks in two.

My mother jumps up. "Oh, no," she says, her hands flying to her mouth. John whips around, totally startled. His face flushes beet-red.

"Oh, gosh, I'm really sorry. I'm such a klutz."

Herman puts his arm around John and leads him toward the hallway. "Now, don't you worry about it, son. It was just an accident." I watch Herman. He's perfectly at ease. You might say he's in his element. People in distress must be his specialty, he's so good at it. No wonder he can deal with my mother.

"I'll pay for the damage, Mrs. Baskowitz," John calls over his shoulder.

"No, no," my mother says. Then she glares at me as if I've just brought a demolition squad into the house. "You look awful. Go change." She gets down on the floor, looking for any remaining slivers.

"It's a clean break, and I'm not changing."

Herman calls from out in the hall, "Roxie, why don't you and John run along."

"I'd love to run along." I affect my most sarcastic voice.

"Roxie," warns Mother. I leave without saying good-bye. Well, it's her fault John stumbled and broke the table. If she were more normal, he wouldn't have felt so weird. I can see my future spread before me: a long line of boys who enter my house of horrors, meet my mother, commit some bizarre act, and then disappear, never to darken my door again.

17

Once we're out, John flings his arms high in the air and shakes his fist at the sky. "Oh, great god of klutziness! Why me?" Then he hurls himself to the ground, letting forth loud wailing noises.

I lean over and pound him on the back, not hard enough to hurt, but with enough force to push him over on the grass. Like a big, silly dog, he sticks his arms and legs up in the air, and then we start laughing and sputtering until we're practically crying. "You were a dope, but worse things could have happened."

"Just wait," he says. "I make a fool of myself at least three times a day."

"You've got two more tries." We bound to our feet and, wiping the grass off our clothes, continue to knock against each other.

"Just two big klutzes on the highway of life."

"Don't feel bad. I once walked through a glass door, smashed it to smithereens."

"You're not as clumsy as I am. I've seen you cavorting

around in Aerobics Eddie's class. For a tall girl, you're not so bad."

"Thanks a lot." Supporting each other, we take long strides down the street. "Keep in step," I say, two beats at a time.

"Rolling home, dead drunk. Rolling home, by the light of the silvery moon. Happy is the day when our parents go away, and we go rolling, rolling home," John sings out.

A light drizzle is falling as we two-step up the misty street. The sky flashes with streaks of lightning. "It's going to pour any minute. Let's run," I say, as I break away from him and race toward number one, which is blazing with lights.

"They're expecting us," John says, catching up.

"I think it's Tony Sansone they're all lit up about. Mrs. Stern calls him the scholarship boy."

Slumped on the front steps is a small figure. As John and I come closer, we recognize the short, husky frame of Tony Sansone himself, hugging his knees and looking extremely tense. "I've been waiting for you." He points behind him. "Man, you could stuff my whole house in their garage."

"We brought Trivial Pursuit along. A little intellectual activity to calm your nerves," says John. Or your overactive hormones, I think.

I bang on the front door a few times, and Glo flings it open. "Darlings," she says. "Come in."

I groan to myself. She's decked out in a one-piece turquoise leotard with red diamonds all over it, and a magenta miniskirt. She looks like a harlequin. Behind her is Mrs. Stern in a gauzy long gown. Beads the size of Christmas-tree ornaments dangle from her ears. "A party. Isn't this fun," she says, swinging her wineglass. "Ray's in New York, so you don't have to worry about making a mess."

The four of us trail behind her, single file, toward the downstairs sitting room. Mrs. Stern leads, with Glo behind, followed by Tony, who's no longer swaggering but rather shuffling. John and I bring up the rear. A strange procession. Next to Glo and her mother, the three of us practically fade into the woodwork.

After her first enthusiasm, Glo falls into a sulk and sinks onto the cushions. She rolls her eyes a few times when I'm the only one looking. Her mother sets a bottle of wine on the coffee table and, spreading out her filmy skirt, settles into an armchair as if she's set for the evening. "When I was your age, we traveled in packs. My mother used to swear she couldn't tell the girls from the boys, because we all had such long hair."

No one else seems to know what to make of this statement, so I decide to jump in. "I love that photograph of you at the peace rally, Mrs. Stern. What did your parents think about that?"

Mrs. Stern props her feet on the ottoman and sips her wine thoughtfully, as if she's conjuring up a half-forgotten memory. "I don't remember them voicing any opinions whatsoever. The truth is, I think they were scared to death of me. They didn't know what to make of the peace marches, the love-ins, sit-ins, and what have you." She laughs, obviously tickled by that old image of herself. "I wandered around in old clothes I picked up in rummage sales, and hung out in public parks, chanting my mantra."

"My mother says that only rich kids want to wear used clothes or have time to loaf in the park," Tony says sullenly. He's chosen the farthest chair from the group and is fiddling with an ashtray.

Mrs. Stern drains her glass and then refills it. She turns to look at Tony as if she's just noticed him for the first time. "Well, I don't think it was a question of being rich or poor. We were just trying to make a statement, assert our individuality. After all, there was a senseless war going on in Vietnam. One of our most popular Presidents had just been assassinated. All our parents preached was success, when the world seemed to be falling apart around us."

"There's nothing wrong with being a success or being able to afford nice clothes," Tony says stubbornly from his corner. "My father didn't have time for politics. He was working all the time." Although Tony's not being rude to Glo's mother, he isn't trying to be pleasant either. Tony's challenging Mrs. Stern, as he does everyone else. The funny thing is, I see his point.

"Well, despite what you may think about our self-indulgent generation, we did accomplish a few things in the area of civil rights, and especially in drawing the public's attention to a useless war."

"My uncle was shot down in 'Nam," says Tony. "He won the Purple Heart. He doesn't think it was a useless war."

John's looking up at the ceiling as if it's projecting an intriguing picture. I'm trying to think of a way to change the subject, and Glo is staring worshipfully in Tony's direction.

Mrs. Stern pulls herself to her feet. "Well, this has been a fascinating discussion," she says to Tony. "You're an interesting young man. Such a wonderful complexion. Your face looks as if it's been brushed by a rosy palette."

In the corner, Tony's rosy palette turns rosier. "Yes, ma'am."

"You must let me do a portrait of you sometime." John stands. "Well, nice to see you, Mrs. Stern."

"Give me a hug, John. A big kiss to your parents. Night, Roxie." Then she whirls around, earrings bobbing, skirt swishing, and disappears down the hall.

"Whew," says John. "That was getting heavy."

Spread out on the pastel pillows, Glo looks like a giant butterfly. I can tell she's pleased by the whole exchange. If Tony wasn't her hero before, he certainly is now. After all, he had a "fascinating" conversation with Maggie and proved he wasn't "boring." His opinions were right in character, as far as I'm concerned. Hostile and arrogant! But I'm sorry Mrs. Stern didn't stick around. What are we going to do now?

"So," I say brightly, "time for a little television?" I flip through the *TV Guide*. "Hmm. Channel 5 has *Attack of the Giant Leeches.*"

"You're kidding," says John, grabbing the magazine. "Let me see. Oh, no, listen to this. 'Blood-sucking creatures rise from the mire of the Everglades and grow attached to careless humans.'"

"How does one rise from the mire?" asks Glo.

"Like this." I squirm my way out of the couch and

wiggle my fingers. Then I hop around, making sucking noises, and end my performance by taking a nosedive. "Gotcha," I croak, zapping into John.

"The giant leech rides again," he says, scooting out of my way. Glo laughs. Tony scowls from his corner.

"Come on, Tony," says John. "Where's your sense of humor?"

"Do you have anything to drink?" Tony asks Glo.

"How about some wine?"

John opens his mouth, then closes it again. "Sure," Tony says, fixing his eyes on John, daring him to object.

Glo skips over to the bar and collects four wineglasses as if she's done this hostess routine a hundred times before.

"Nothing for me," I say primly. John shakes his head, too.

"Two old grouches," Glo says.

Tony and Glo click glasses and gulp their wine. He stretches out on the cushion next to her. When he takes off his letter jacket, I realize he's gotten over his earlier nervousness. A bad sign.

"Let's play Trivial Pursuit," I say. I glance at John.

"Terrific idea," he says. "I should have thought of it myself. As a matter of fact, we happen to have a set right here."

"I hate board games. I'm terrible at them," Glo objects, pouring Tony another glass of wine. I'm relieved to see there's not much left in the bottle.

Tony props himself up on his elbows. "No problem. I'll help you."

"Promise?" she says, practically batting her eyelashes.

We unfold the board and choose our tokens, each taking a turn rolling the dice.

"I've got five, the highest number," announces John. "I go first." He lands on the green space, Science and Nature. "I'm terrific at that."

"What's 'triskaidekaphobia'?" I say, reading from the card.

John scratches his head. "That's an absurd question."

"Talk a lot between moves," I whisper to him.

"Hey, no coaching," says Tony.

"Wait a minute," says Glo. "You promised to help me."

"The rules don't apply to you," says Tony, ruffling her hair. This produces a wildly happy smile from Glo.

"You're not telling her anything she doesn't know already," I say crossly.

"Hey, now," Glo protests. "That's not very nice."

"John, answer the question," I order.

"I give up." He grabs the card. "Fear of the number 13. I should have known that."

"And today is Friday the 13th," I remind him.

"This is the most annoying game," grumbles Glo. "How about some more wine."

"Why not," says Tony.

"Don't open another bottle," I say. "Your mother will find out, and then we'll all be in trouble."

"By now she's sound asleep, dreaming of Julio," says Glo, giggling. "Don't worry about a thing."

"My turn," she tells Tony, rolling the dice. She moves to green.

"What age is adolescence considered to end at?" reads Tony.

"Fifteen," she says, twisting the corkscrew into the bottle.

"Hardly," says John. "You've still got a few more years to go."

"Not tonight." She gives me a defiant look, and I get the impression she's showing off for Tony and trying to annoy me at the same time. "Well, I don't think we have to sit around all night and play this boring game. It'll be midnight before anyone comes close to winning," she says.

"I bet you're wrong," Tony tells her. He hands John the box of question cards. "Here, ask me anything."

"Which category?"

"Doesn't matter." He springs up and begins to strut around the room, picking up an ashtray, a table lighter, then putting them down, circling the room like a lion on the prowl. They're both showing off for each other.

"What number is at six o'clock on the dartboard?" begins John.

"Three," says Tony.

"What's the capital of Iceland?"

"Reykjavik," he says. "I know that because I did my history report on countries in the Frigid Zones." He's still circling, sipping, grinning at Glo as if she's south of the Equator.

"What's the cube root of 64?"

"Easy," says the genius. "Four."

"That *was* easy." My remark produces a black look from Glo.

And so it goes, until he misses four tries later with "What oath begins with 'I swear by Apollo the physician'?"

"Give up?" John says. "The Hippocratic Oath. I know that one because my father's a doctor."

"So big deal," says Tony. "Not everybody's father's a doctor."

"Hey, get off my back," says John. "C'mon, buddy, the wine must be getting to you."

For no reason at all, Tony makes a fist and punches the wall. Then it dawns on me that I don't really like Tony Sansone. I don't like waiting for him every morning on the bus. I don't like the way he bullies the other kids, as if the world owes him. As far as I can tell, he has a lot going for him—why is he so surly?

At that point, Glo says, "I feel sick," and darts out. Tony pulls his jacket off the couch and races after her.

John says, "Maybe Trivial Pursuit wasn't such a hot idea."

"Sure it was. Now I know what triskaidekaphobia means." We both laugh nervously. "If Glo's right and adolescence actually does end at fifteen, we're in big trouble," I say, going over to the window.

For a while I stare out into the darkness. Rain pours like a waterfall down the glass panes. The pine trees sway and shiver. Two figures dart across the lawn, the lightning cracking all around them—Glo and Tony hurling themselves through the storm.

"Oh, no. Look at those two idiots!" John rushes over in time to see them reach the Sterns' Cadillac and climb in. A second later, the headlights pop on and the car creeps off, fading into the night. John's face must mirror my own, a mixture of horror and helplessness.

"Who's driving?"

I shake my head, but I have a horrible premonition.

"Should we find Mrs. Stern?" John asks.

"Let's wait. Maybe they'll be right back. Why don't we clean up." But when I pick up the bottle and glasses, my hands are shaking.

"Are you okay?" John takes them from me and stashes the bottle in the waste can. While I wash out the wine glasses, my imagination starts running wild. "They might kill themselves, or someone else."

"That would be the worst thing that could happen," he tells me. "Let's work up from there."

"Maybe we'd better not talk about it." I say.

John and I huddle on the couch. I close my eyes and lean against him. "You're trembling," he says, putting his arm around me. It's comfortable, and when I put my head on his shoulder, I realize no one has held me close for a long time. Not since my dad died. I squeeze my eyes to hold back the tears, feeling warm inside, but sad at the same time.

But I can't hold on to that feeling for long because I start thinking about Glo and Tony again. "I knew Glo shouldn't get mixed up with someone like Tony," I say, clenching my thumbs.

"What do you mean?" John removes his arm and turns to face me. "Tony's a good guy."

"Oh, he's terrific. Mr. Macho himself. I can't figure out what she sees in him." I picture Tony in my mind, the dark eyes, the cocky stance.

"All the girls like Tony. They crawl all over him."

"But Glo deserves someone better. She's not used to being with his type." I can hear my voice as if it were my mother's, articulating each word. "Either are you. Why do you hang out with him?"

"Listen, just because his dad runs a gas station and his house is a little shabby doesn't give you the right to put him down."

"I know. I know. Who do I think I am?" I remember Mrs. Stern calling him the scholarship boy, and how Mr. Stern turns his nose up at me. Now I'm acting the same way. "Maybe I'm being snobby. But there's more to it than that. He's just a troublemaker," I insist.

"Glo's not so innocent, either. How do you know the car thing wasn't her idea? She's the one who started with the wine."

"Maybe so, but I didn't see Tony object. He's the worst trasher I've ever met," I say, knowing that I'm wrong.

"Now you sound like my mother, the Chief of Protocol. You should hear her lectures on manners and morals."

"But you know how to act. Tony doesn't. Why did he get so hot and bothered with you? You're supposed to be his buddy."

"He didn't want me to outshine him in front of Glo."

"What a ridiculous ego! And did you see the way he tried to pick a fight with Mrs. Stern?"

"He doesn't mean to stir up trouble. But he's a person with definite opinions. That's another reason I like Tony. Nobody can push him around."

"Oh, I get it. Tony's a rebel. That's what turns Glo on, too."

John squeezes me. "Oh, yes. Chalk it up to the old rebellious teenager act."

"Well, you can joke all you want. But that's exactly

what this is about. And now Glo's gone too far." I'm getting angrier. "And what are we supposed to do? Sit here and wait, totally freaked out, while Tony and Glo go on a joyride?"

"We don't have much choice," says John. "There are definite sparks between those two."

"I'll never go for someone just because he makes me quiver. It's stupid." I move away from him and kick the ottoman.

"How come you're so tough?"

"I've had to be. Did I tell you about my rotten childhood?" I use a flippant tone, but the truth is, I'm serious. Glo hasn't had a hard moment in her whole life.

"You know something, Roxie? I don't think you're as tough as you act. And neither is Tony. You should see him at home. It doesn't matter how late he stays at school playing ball or how much homework he has. His dad still expects him to put in twenty hours a week at the station and to help with his little brothers. I don't think taking the Sterns' car was right, but I still respect him for other things."

"Well, then, we have a difference of opinion. But the fact remains that they're still out there in the storm, and we don't know what's happening."

We grow silent, pressed together on the couch. Maybe we even fall asleep, because when the phone rings, we both jump up, startled. "Wait for Mrs. Stern to answer it," John says.

Ten rings later, he finally grabs the receiver. "Hello," he begins in a strong voice, but gradually his responses grow weaker. Holding his hand over the mouthpiece, he turns to me. "You'd better wake Mrs. Stern. They're holding Glo and Tony at the police station." He hits his head with the palm of his hand. "Those idiots ran into a tree."

"Are they all right?" He nods. I race upstairs to the Sterns' bedroom. "Mrs. Stern," I shout, knocking on the door. No answer. Finally, I barge in. She's spread out, fully dressed, on top of the covers. "Mrs. Stern," I repeat, then louder, but she doesn't budge. Tapping her shoulder, I feel the bones, sharp beneath her dress, and smell a fruity aroma of wine. Her lipstick is smeared, her eye makeup smudged. She looks unreal, like one of those mannequins in a wax museum.

"Hmmmmm," she murmurs, turning over. I try again, but she's out of it.

"Hurry," comes John's voice from downstairs. "The cop wants to speak to Glo's mother."

I pick up the phone next to Maggie's bed and try to sound mature. "Sir, Mrs. Stern isn't available at the present moment, but we'll straighten this out immediately."

"Who is this?" demands the voice on the other end. "We need an adult at the station, or these two are going to spend the night in Juvenile Hall."

"Don't worry, there'll be an adult," I say. I hear John take a deep breath. Then I hang up.

He's upstairs in two seconds, staring down at Maggie. "My parents are in New York for a medical convention," he says.

"I can't call my mother. She won't know what to do. She can't handle a situation like this."

"You're going to have to. Who else is there?"

"Maybe we should wait for Irene and your brother to get in?"

"Are you crazy? Irene will have a fit. Besides, the cops want an adult."

"Maggie, Maggie," I say, shaking her. She flings her arm over her head.

"It's no use," John says. "She's out like a light." He hands me the phone. "Call your mother."

18

It doesn't take Mother more than two minutes to drive up to Glo's. When she honks, we run out to the car. The rain has stopped, and the air is heavy and damp. I splash right into a puddle, completely soaking my shoes, but she doesn't say anything when water drips all over the floor of the car.

John climbs in the back seat and slams the door so hard the car shakes. "Oops. Sorry," he says. Polite even in moments of crisis.

"Where's Herman?" I ask, wishing for once he was with her.

"He went home."

"Why don't we pick up Aunt Dorothy?" I'm starting to panic.

"I will do this," my mother says adamantly. "So?"

"I don't know if they wrecked the car or not," I tell her, "but the police are holding them until we get there."

"This is awful" are the only words she utters all the way downtown to the police station. I wonder how she's going to deal with the police. As Mother steers the car through the fog, the city seems unusually dark; the street lamps and neon signs cast an eerie glow over the slick streets.

The station is one of those one-story modern buildings, cream brick, with sliding glass doors, and a smell of disinfectant inside. Rows of folding metal chairs line the lobby. At a counter, a woman in a blue uniform stands busily writing. As soon as we announce ourselves, she presses a button on the wall. I look around, but I don't see Glo and Tony. Then a police officer emerges from a back room and strides toward us. "Mrs. Stern?"

"Frances Baskowitz," my mother says, enunciating each syllable. "Mrs. Stern is sick."

Stiff as sentries, John and I flank her. "We're their friends," I add. "Are they okay?"

"They're a little shook up," says the officer. "Apparently, the boy"—he looks down at his chart—"Tony Sansone, was driving when the car skidded around a turn. He lost control and went into a tree. They're lucky they didn't get killed. He flunked the breath test." I throw John a furious, knowing look.

"I will take them home," my mother says very firmly.

"The little girl's in bad shape, too. Keeps throwing up."

"She's not drunk," I say defensively. "She's very upset."

"Sure," the officer says. He turns to Mother. "We have to file a report on this, ma'am. They'll be getting a letter from juvenile court in a few weeks."

"What's going to happen to them?" I blurt, picturing

Glo and Tony behind bars in some dingy cell crawling with rats.

"It's up to the judge. In the boy's case, probably a detention or restriction on his driver's license until he's eighteen. That's for openers." He sounds bored, as if he's been through this a hundred times before. He hands Mother a piece of paper. "Sign this form, but we can't promise to send them home with you. The regulations specify a parent or an attorney. The boy's father refused to come down here." I detect a faint smirk when he adds, "He said, 'Let him rot in jail'."

"I see," says my mother, raising her eyebrows.

"May we talk to them?" asks John. He clutches my hand. To reassure him, I squeeze back.

"Sure, go on in there while Mrs. Baskowitz and I discuss a few details." He gestures toward the door. My mother stands very straight. Something about her manner causes me to stay right where I am, to watch what she does next.

"I will take . . . home," she announces. "Now."

The policeman shakes his head. "Wrecking a car. Driving while intoxicated. No license. Under age. This is pretty serious business." Confused by Mother's overbearing style, he doesn't understand yet that it's the only way she can communicate.

"They are not . . ." she stutters, trying to say the right word, "not . . . bad."

"Excuse me, m'am?" He's having trouble following her. I tighten my grip on John's hand, my heart pounding. "Now, what exactly is your relationship to these youngsters?"

"My girl." She points to me. "They are friends." He peers at me quizzically. What's this lady's problem, I read in his eyes. If I could jump in and rescue Mother, save her from another humiliating experience, I would. But I know he wouldn't listen to me. Why didn't she bring Aunt Dorothy?

"We go to school together," I offer weakly.

"Bannister Prep," adds John.

"They are good kids," my mother insists. "They will come with me." She points to herself, cocks her head as if to say, "Come on, you know what I mean." And I realize how hard this is for her, but my mother refuses to be intimidated. And for the first time I'm right there in her corner, rooting for her, proud of the way she's handling this. I know she's struggling, but she's not backing down. And somehow, with all her fumbling, she's making her point.

The policeman looks from John to me, and back to my mother. "Bannister Prep. I see."

I feel the tears well up in my eyes. Mother's trying so hard. And it's for me. I know that, too. And if I didn't understand the meaning of dignity before, I know it now. My mother, standing there in her wet raincoat, laboring to find the right words, is dignified—and wonderful.

"I think you're right, Mrs. Baskowitz," he says, relenting. "Let's do the paperwork and you can take them home." She nods as if to confirm he's made the correct decision. Then, when she glances over at me, I shoot her the victory signal and a big smile.

"Let's go see Glo and Tony," John says to me softly.

We find them sitting on opposite sides of a small office.

Furnished with a metal desk, a file cabinet, and a couple of chairs, it could be an office anywhere, except for the "Most Wanted Men" poster tacked on the wall. Glo whimpers, while Tony is hunched over, a grim look on his face. I rush to Glo, John to Tony.

"Roxie, is Mother here?" Her nose is running, her eyes puffy. She wipes her face on her sleeve and sniffles.

"She's, uh . . . well, she's in bed. I couldn't wake her. I guess she's, uh, sick."

"Oh, no," moans Glo, lowering her head. "Don't ever tell anyone about her, Roxie. I mean it."

"Don't worry. I won't, Glo. I promise. My mother's here. Now tell me, what happened?" I glance at Tony. He's just sitting there, not saying a word to John, who's wearing a helpless expression.

Glo sneaks a quick glance at Tony, but it isn't her usual adoring look. This time her face registers fear. I could just throttle him, I'm so angry. She rests her arm on mine, her head turned away from the boys. "What did the police tell you?" Her breath gives off a sour, nasty odor.

"Let's go into the bathroom and clean you up," I say. Unwilling to let Tony hear our conversation, I steer Glo out of the office. We go across the reception area toward the ladies room. Over Glo's shoulder, I see my mother at the counter. She's not smiling—but why would she be? Irene once told us she charmed a policeman out of giving her a speeding ticket, but my mother doesn't resort to those tricks. "Don't worry," I tell Glo. "Tony's the one who's in trouble, not you. He didn't pass the breath test, and the police know he was driving."

Glo coughs and gags. Then she says in a low voice,

"That's just it, Roxie. He wasn't driving." I blink at her, a terrible coldness creeping over me.

"What do you mean?"

"I mean," says Glo, her voice shaking, "that he's taking the blame for me. You know how my father is. If he finds out, I'll never hear the end of it."

"But what about Tony's father? He told the police to let Tony rot in jail." Glo doesn't answer. Now I'm the one who's queasy. "How can you let him do that?"

Glo splashes water on her face and dries off with a paper towel. She gives me a piercing stare, her expression hard. She's absolutely in control when she snaps, "That's between him and me," and marches out, leaving me staring after her, my head spinning. I don't know what to do next, so I go into one of the stalls and sink down on the toilet. I just sit there staring at the tile wall.

What seems like hours later, my mother pushes through the door. "We can go, Roxie," she says. Numbly, I follow her. It's drizzling, and the street is empty except for two squad cars and our Buick. Then I spot the Sterns' white Cadillac across the street in the parking lot. The front end is totally bent out of shape, squashed in and crinkled like one of Aunt Dorothy's discarded pages. Glo, Tony, and John pile into the back seat of our car. John's in the middle. I slide in front, next to my mother, facing straight ahead. No one says a word.

19

In the middle of the night, I awaken all tangled in the
sheets, wet with perspiration. The room is stifling, as if
the muggy night air has seeped through the windows to
enclose me. My head throbs. I kick off the covers and
change to a fresh T-shirt. Then I lie down and try to fall
asleep again.

I'm on the Bannister bus. Glo sits next to me, yelling
at the driver. "Go faster. Go faster." I look behind me,
to see Tony chasing the bus. His little brothers scramble
alongside. And suddenly I'm racing down the road with
Tony. I see my mother's face next to Glo's, staring out
the back window of the bus. No matter how fast we run,
we can't catch up, until finally the bus pulls way ahead
and disappears.

I open my eyes, out of breath and gasping for air. My
bedroom is washed in the pale morning light. When I
lean my head out the window and inhale, I see the sun
dimly through gray clouds. The first day of spring vacation—dismal! I blow out, emptying my lungs with a

long, whirring sound. From below comes a loud thumping noise. I look down to see Merlie practicing her backhand against the garage door. What's she doing up so early, I wonder. But when I check my alarm clock I see it's past eleven. For a while I watch Merlie. She hardly ever misses, whacking the ball steadily with total concentration. I wonder if she knows what went on last night. Then I wonder if the Sterns are still going to Sarasota for their vacation today. How can Glo leave, knowing it's her fault Tony's in so much trouble? Is she going to Florida to stick her head in the sand and ignore what she's left behind? But I can't disregard what's happened or look the other way. What to do next? Maybe Merlie has the right idea, throwing herself into physical exercise. Aerobics Eddie says it's a sure way to forget your troubles. I tug on my sweats and drag myself downstairs to go jogging.

My mother is standing in the kitchen, speaking slowly into the phone. "It was awful," she says to someone, probably my Aunt Dorothy. "No, I did." She stumbles over a word a few times, followed by "He is a bad boy." As soon as I realize she's trying to say Sansone, I know I can't leave the house without talking to her.

I hang by the door until she's through. "Mother, can I speak to you for a second?"

She narrows her eyes with the slightest flicker of surprise. Usually, when I have something to say, I approach her like a bulldozer. She pulls out a chair and sits, motioning me to join her at the table. "Here." She pours me a glass of orange juice. "How is Glo? You have talked to her?"

I shake my head. "She and her family are probably on their way to Florida by now." I gulp the juice, its cold, acidy taste clearing the tightness in my throat.

"So?" She pats my hand.

"About last night . . ."

"I was good. See?" Mother nods expectantly, her head tilted, shoulders erect. I can tell she's feeling up today . . . which lets me know how often my mother must feel down. How can I tell her the real story and spoil the pride she's feeling about herself? Instead of answering, I shrug and automatically pull my hand away.

"Oh, Roxie," comes the familiar hurt tone and the shadow of sadness in her eyes.

I didn't mean to act mean, I want to say; instead, I blurt, "You just don't know."

"*You* don't know," she says. Clenching her fists, she pulls herself up heavily and walks out of the kitchen, leaving me feeling like a brat again. And this time my intentions were good. It always works out the same way between Mother and me. One moment a door opens, and the next it slams shut and leaves us on opposite sides. Each time there's a chance to meet halfway, I mess up, say something wrong, and the door closes again. It goes on and on this way.

But I can't sit here brooding. She's going to find out sooner or later that she rescued the wrong person. And Glo—what am I going to do about her?

At that moment my Aunt Dorothy breezes in, swinging her red shoulder bag, looking pleased with the world. I practically leap out of my chair with relief. She'll know how to handle this. "I hear your mother saved the day," she starts out. "Aren't you proud?"

"Yes, but . . ." This isn't going to be easy.

"Well, I hope you told her, for God's sake. Even a mother needs a little encouragement." She puts her hands on my shoulders and gives me a nudge. "Especially my sister."

"Sorry to disappoint you. But I acted like my usual bratty self, and we ended up in a fight again."

She leads me outside. We stand together on the porch. "Why?"

In a jumble of words, I explain what happened last night, at least the part I know for sure—the drinking, Tony and Glo taking off in the car, and later what she admitted in the ladies' room. My aunt listens, her mouth fixed in a thin line—knitting her eyebrows at the last part. "I started to tell Mother but couldn't. I blew it again and hurt her feelings. Ohhh, I am awful, just like she says."

"Sometimes you do act awful. But that doesn't mean your mother thinks you're an awful person." Aunt Dorothy faces me, standing so close I'm aware of how much taller I am. I stoop over a little.

"Yes, she does. I don't blame her. Only a horrible person acts mean to someone who's sick."

"Roxie, it's not your fault Franny got sick. What do you want to do, walk around your whole life feeling horrible because sometimes—like everyone in the world who has a mother, handicapped or normal—you fight with her?"

"No, but I get so angry. You say 'be nice,' but I can't

control my anger when she criticizes me or won't talk."

"It's normal to fight. Maybe I've forgotten what it's like to be fifteen." She shakes her head. "Stop feeling so guilty. You didn't want to disappoint her about last night. You were proud of her. I can see that. You just slipped into that old pattern you two have of misunderstanding each other."

A long sigh runs through me. "So?" I say, the way Mother does.

Aunt Dorothy smiles. "Go back and talk it out. Tell her I'll call later." With that, she reaches up and ruffles my hair. "You're not half as bad as you think you are."

In the end, my mother has only one thing to say. "This is not right. You go talk to Glo." Then she reaches out and touches my cheek, and somehow her slow, emphatic tone and the light gesture comfort me. I know that this time we've opened that stubborn door.

20

Out on the street, I take full, rapid strides uphill to Glo's, pushing my body forward until all my energy is directed toward moving ahead. When her house comes into view, gaping cheerfully down from the hill, I notice four or five cars in front. With a sinking feeling, I stop running to catch my breath. What's going on? Cautiously, I ring the bell. A few minutes later, Charles answers the door. I hear voices in the background. "Whew, is this house bedlam today," he says. "You'd better come in and keep Glo company. She's in mighty sorry shape." Did someone die? Why does Glo need company?

The dining-room table is laden with cookies, indicating some kind of party. But when I glimpse the people milling about with somber faces, I realize this isn't a festive occasion. Mr. Stern is slumped on the couch, surrounded by the Lessers, Buffy's parents, and some other people I've seen here once or twice before. "Where's Glo?" I ask, and Charles points upstairs.

I find her face-down on her bed. "Glo, are you all right?"

She rolls over and stares up at me with bloodshot eyes. "They've sent Maggie away."

"Sent her away? Where did she go?" Thank goodness no one's dead.

"Dad came home early this morning. Mother was sick again, and it wasn't even nine o'clock. He called Dr. Lesser, and they bundled her up and took her away."

"What do you mean?"

Glo jerks to a sitting position. "You know what I mean," she says, almost accusingly. "She was drunk, and they took her to a sanatorium to dry out. Cherry Hill, it's called. In Concord, New Hampshire." Glo crosses her legs and leans against the pillow. "Dad's been threatening to send her there for months."

"Why didn't you tell me?" I sit down on the edge of the bed and reach over to take her hand. Her fingers are ice-cold, and she moves her hand away.

"Dad said we had to protect her, tell people she was sick, but lately it hasn't been easy to hide. She's been acting up a lot." I nod, remembering her condition last night. "This has been going on for a long time," she says bitterly. "When her friends started making remarks, I knew something was going to break. Buffy's mother went shopping with her last week and told my dad she was wearing her dress inside out. And then Mother fell asleep at the table in the middle of a dinner party the other night."

"Your mother's a terrific person. I know she'll pull through this."

"My dad said she never grew up. He says she was just a child when they got married. People have always taken care of her, so she became more and more helpless, more and more dependent. Well, maybe she'll get better now. Maybe my dad will stop being so mean to her." Tears spill down Glo's cheeks. "I've been so nervous about her and my dad," she continues, "that I always feel sick to my stomach."

"I'm really sorry." I don't know what else to say. In the back of my mind nags the subject that I can't avoid. If I leave without confronting her, I know I'll regret it later. I move closer. "So, what are you going to do about Tony?" My voice sounds muffled, forced from the back of my throat.

She flicks her hair back. "I can't do anything about him right now. I have enough to worry about."

"But Tony's in terrible trouble," I tell her. "What about juvenile court?"

Glo twists away and goes over to her dresser. She begins to comb her hair, pulling the teeth through her tangled curls with slow, determined strokes. "I'm just not ready to deal with that."

"Does your dad know about last night?"

"Of course he does. Our car's all bashed in. But right now, making arrangements for Mother is more important." She sets the comb down but doesn't turn to face me.

"Glo," I say, "I'm not sure I can let you do this."

Still looking into the mirror, she says firmly, "It's up to Tony. You weren't even there."

I pause at the door. "I'm really sorry about your

mother. You say she's become helpless. Do you figure you're any different if you let Tony take the blame for what you did?" Then I close the door softly and make my way downstairs and out the front door.

21

My eyes start watering and I realize I'm standing outside with the sun glaring in my eyes. I remember the way I used to stare at the sun, hoping to be transformed into a beautiful princess. Maybe that's why Maggie Stern loved the sun; she secretly wanted to turn into someone else. Funny, I don't believe in the magic of the sun anymore, and as for being transformed, I think I'll stick to being me. Blinking from the glare, I turn in the other direction.

Two squirrels move toward me in darts and pauses, their rat-like mouths open expectantly. "I have nothing to give you," I tell them as they scurry past.

"Talking to the squirrels?" comes a voice. "Do you do that a lot?"

I glance down the hill to see John trotting toward me with a big grin on his face.

"I think I'm in a trance," I say. "I'm totally weirded out."

"Have you been to see Glo?" he asks, not smiling anymore.

"Yes, and it wasn't very pleasant, but I guess you know what's going on there. So, go on inside and be sympathetic." I don't even try to disguise my scorn. What I'm really thinking is that he and that whole group will rally around the Sterns. They're all for sticking together, and if they do find out what happened last night between Glo and Tony, Mr. Stern and the rest will probably try to cover it up.

"Actually, I came to find you, Roxie," John says, to my complete surprise. "I went by your house, and your mom told me you were here." He looks down and nudges a rock with the toe of his sneaker. "I couldn't sleep all night."

"I had trouble myself. Horrible dreams."

John takes my elbow and steers me toward the street. "I want to go by Tony's. He wouldn't talk to me last night, but I know from past experience that he's in deep trouble at home. His father's a tyrant." He stuffs his hands into his pockets as we both trudge off. Observing his look, I realize that since we're in this together, I ought to trust him.

The sky is almost white, and there's a light drizzle. Somewhere the sun has disappeared behind the haze. At Lindbergh Boulevard, the light turns green. As we cross, I say to John, "Glo's letting Tony take the blame for her. She was driving."

John stops dead in his tracks. "I should have known," he said, knocking his palm on his head. "What do we do now?"

The lights change again, and cars are inching toward us, honking. "The first thing we have to do is cross the street without being run over." We grab hands and race to the other side. John is still holding my hand as we proceed around the corner. Funny thing is that it feels good.

When the wood-frame houses on the dead end come into view, I tell John, "From *my* past experience with Tony, he's the most difficult boy in town, not to mention the most macho. How're we going to convince him that he doesn't need to defend a damsel in distress at his own expense?"

"Let's just be cool and see what happens," suggests John. "All I want to do is let him know I'm in his corner."

"Okay." Suddenly I feel leery about going inside. The front of the house reminds me of the face of a goblin, with gray menacing clouds behind it. The roof slants down, and the windows droop. The door, with its broken screen, looks like a mouth curved into a frown.

A dark, plump woman with the blackest eyes I've ever seen answers the door. She smiles when she recognizes John. "Come in," she says, in a heavy accent. "My Tony, he is an unhappy boy today."

"I smell homemade bread, Mrs. Sansone," says John.

"Well, it's Saturday, isn't it? I make enough for the whole week."

"Tony's mom makes the best sourdough in the whole world," John says to me. She looks over, brushing the wisps of hair off her face, which is full and rosy, like Tony's. "This is Roxie Baskowitz," John says. I hold out my hand. She wipes hers on her apron and then shakes mine.

"Such a pretty girl." She gives John a wink. I hunch up my shoulders, and John looks pained. Sensing our discomfort, she quickly ushers us in. "My husband is in the kitchen. He's very angry today." She wrings her hands.

We're standing in a small, square hall. The floor is painted blue, and on it is a small, tattered rug. We follow her into a room filled with old-fashioned furniture—heavy, stuffed chairs, a brown couch, and carved mahogany tables. There are riding toys, games, and newspapers strewn everywhere. Even though the place looks messy and lived in, it's clean.

In the midst of all this sprawls Tony, who looks as if he's seen better days, too. His clothes are rumpled, as if he's slept in them. From some other part of the house, a little boy yells, and the television squawks Saturday-cartoon talk. Tony hardly acknowledges our presence. He pretends to be studying his math book. John collapses on the couch, and I follow suit. No one says anything. The silence seems to lengthen, and the room grows smaller.

"Maybe boys sit around and wait for something to happen," I say finally, "but this girl doesn't." Tony looks up from his book and scowls, but I press on. "Tony, I don't know all the details about last night, but John and I nearly went crazy with worry, and we're still crazy."

"Forget about it," mumbles Tony. Then he sighs. "Listen, Glo and I didn't mean to run off and desert you, but, well, she was all upset. She needed to get out of the house. I guess we were a little trashed."

"You don't have to protect Glo," I say. "That's the last thing she needs. She should face up to her own mistakes."

"You don't know Glo," he says huskily. "She's so
. . . so helpless." She's not helpless, I want to say. She just
thinks she is. But I keep still.

"What if you're kicked out of Bannister?" asks John.

"Well, it's not the greatest place in the world," Tony
says. But I can tell by the way he won't look us in the
eye that he feels just the opposite. "I never met a girl like
Glo," he says softly. "She's like a china doll, all bright and
shining. I can't hurt her. I'll take my chances."

John and I exchange hopeless looks. There are no
chances in a situation like this.

"What's going on?" A loud voice interrupts us. At
the doorway looms a dark, wiry man, bald, wearing a
T-shirt and gray pants covered with oil stains. His nose
looks flattened against his wide face, and his small,
close-set eyes dart from John to me suspiciously. "Stand
up when I speak to you," he growls at Tony, waving a
coffee mug.

"Nothing's going on," Tony says wearily, lifting himself up.

"Hey, John boy," says Mr. Sansone. "Did you hear
what this fine fellow of mine did? This smart scholarship
boy who goes to a fancy school?" He grunts his words
as if he's joking and serious at the same time.

"Okay, Pop," pleads Tony, shrinking in the presence
of this man who's even smaller in size than he is.

"Now I gotta fix some rich girl's Cadillac and take my
son to juvenile court. What did we do to deserve this?"
He moves toward Tony.

John leaps to his feet. "Mr. Sansone, please. You don't
know the whole story." Tony shakes his head in warning.

His father slams his coffee cup on the table, and Tony slumps down and buries his head in his hands. His shoulders shake in soundless crying.

Behind them I see Mrs. Sansone, her arms clasping Tony's little brothers as if to restrain them. "That's enough. The boy's had enough."

At the sound of her voice, Mr. Sansone takes a step back. When he looks at his wife, his face seems to soften. "All right. All right," he says in a resigned voice. Then he turns to John and me. "You kids go on home."

Next to John now, our arms touching, I can feel him shaking, or maybe it's me. "Don't worry, Tony," says John. Then he leads me toward the hall, calling over his shoulder, "We'll be here for you."

It's raining hard now. John and I stumble down the wet pavement. "Let's duck in here," he says, pulling me to a metal bus shelter. The rain clatters over our heads as if coins were dropping from the sky. On the bench, John pulls me so close that my head rests on his shoulder.

"From one crisis to another," I say. "Is that what life is all about, a series of disasters we have no control over? Just stumbling about until the next one strikes?"

Water streams down the sides of the shelter, and cars plod through the flooded streets. Any minute, tires could skid. Without warning, an accident could happen.

"Crises are inevitable," John says slowly, "whether it's an earthquake or an assassination, or illness or death. You can't avoid them."

Now I feel like exploding. "Glo's mother gets sent off to a sanatorium; Tony gets expelled from school. What difference does it make? Just one more personal loss to add to a long list."

"Oh, Roxie. I know what you're saying. I really do. But I can't look at life that way. If we all went around not caring, not even trying to help, the world would really fall apart."

"All right," I say, looking at him. "That makes sense. So, how do we help Tony without hurting Glo?"

"She hurt herself," says John grimly. "That's the way I see it. But I'm not sure about the next step." He puts a wet hand on my cheek. "Look, let's get our minds off them for a while. My dad says the best way to solve a problem is to get some space from it by doing something else, some kind of activity."

"So what should we do?"

"We could make out." My mouth kind of drops open. "Don't laugh." John scoots over away from me, sticking his head between his hands, elbows on his knees.

"No, no. I-er-wasn't going to. Actually, it's not such a bad idea." In the back of my mind, I've been wondering about kissing John, ever since last night on the couch.

"Really?" He brightens.

"Uh-huh."

So cautiously he moves back. Then he leans over and plants a kiss on my lips. We stay that way for a while, our mouths pressed together, and I wait for a quiver. Nothing much happens except that a warm sensation spreads through me. After we finally pull away, I say, "I wonder if this is the kind of activity your father meant."

"Hardly, you nut." We kiss again, this time with more authority. Actually, I wouldn't mind if it rains all day.

22

Each morning over spring break, I've called Glo. I always ask how she's doing, but I don't mention Tony. I wait for her to bring up the subject. She never does. When she tells me to come over, I say no. "Buffy's been such a good friend. She's here constantly." I make no comment. I end the phone calls with "I'm thinking of you." I want Glo to understand that, but I refuse to act as if nothing's changed.

One morning, Buffy answered the phone. "Glo's busy. She can't come to the phone." Then a click, and the line went dead.

Glo and I haven't been together, but John's been coming over every day. Mother says he's turning into a permanent fixture around the house. "He is a nice boy," she keeps telling me. That may not sound like an exciting summation of someone's qualifications, but from my mother it's practically a Nobel Prize.

"Maybe some of that niceness will rub off on you," remarked my Aunt Dorothy. But then she winked, letting me know she was kidding. They both seem pleased that I have a boyfriend.

The other permanent fixture, Herman Levin, turned out not to be so permanent. "We are still friends" was all my mother would say when he stopped coming around. I'd actually gotten used to his honking laugh and long stories, but Aunt Dorothy confided that it was too hard for my mother. "She isn't the same girl he used to know at Soldan High. Trying to talk to him made her frustrated." I guess he became frustrated, too. I hope she finds someone else.

We've been painting my house together, John and me. "I want to do it, too," whined Merlie.

"It's like Tom Sawyer's fence," I told Mother. "Everybody wants to get into the act."

"This is definitely an activity your father would approve of," I told John.

"I like our other activity better," he replied.

"Me, too." But I like talking to John even more. And we never run out of things to say.

By Sunday night, we'd almost finished the entrance hall. Mother stood back and surveyed our job. "This is good."

"I hope this makes up for the table, Mrs. B.," said John. She laughed.

I've decided the smell of new paint is like the aroma of fresh bread—it says someone cares. I keep thinking of Mrs. Sansone, hoping she's holding things together for Tony.

That night, Buffy called. "Something's wrong with

Glo," she said. "She lies in bed all day with a stomach-ache."

"She's upset about her mother," I said, not wanting to betray Glo.

"I may be dense," Buffy remarked, "but there's more to it than that." That's when I wrote a letter to Maggie Stern. *Read this right away,* I wrote on the back of the envelope, and mailed it. But I didn't tell anyone—not even John.

23

The first day back at school, I didn't run into Glo. She wasn't on the bus. We didn't have any classes together and at lunch I went down to the Primary School. Guess who showed up to observe my fitness class? Aunt Dorothy and Mother—all decked out in proper PTA-type suits. My aunt must have convinced Mother that she ought to watch her oldest daughter in action. As soon as Eddie spotted them, he insisted they kick off their high heels and join the circle of screaming six-year-olds. We were attempting to lead them in a jazz routine to Tina Turner singing "What's Love Got to Do with It?"

"Everything," remarked Aunt Dorothy, looking over at me from her position in the middle of the circle, the little ones tugging at her hands from both sides.

"Middle-aged sag and jet lag are the two major diseases of the twentieth century," Eddie informed them. The first-grade teacher nearly fell off her chair. He followed this remark with "But I can see neither of you ladies is fighting the battle of the bulge." Aunt Dorothy blushed.

After that, she and Mother actually got into the swing of things. I won't say they let loose and swung from the rafters, but they bopped around the room a few times and laughed a lot.

After my Pied Piper finale, Mother said, "Roxie, you were good." She never gives a compliment if she doesn't mean it, so maybe she thinks there's hope for me after all. At the end of the session, Eddie handed Aunt Dorothy his card, and she promised to join his Golden Oldies workout at the Y.

24

Today after school, Tony is scheduled to appear in juvenile court. Mother, John, and I have decided to attend the hearing. I wonder if Glo even knows what's happening, if she'll show up at all. Glo avoided me all week. She tilts her nose up when she walks past me now, as if I'm nonexistent. I approached her once, but she tucked her arm through Buffy's and turned away. She's stayed clear of Tony, too. Sometimes I catch him following her with his eyes, but the message is obvious. She doesn't want to have anything to do with him, either. I keep remembering how isolated I felt after my dad died. Without her mother, Glo must be feeling the same way. John told me to stop finding excuses for her behavior.

After the bell, he and I meet on the steps in front of school, and wait for Mother to pick us up. He's wearing a coat and tie instead of his usual T-shirt and baseball cap. "You look as if you're going for an interview at Princeton instead of juvenile court."

"I don't think I can keep my mouth shut any longer," John says.

148

"What can we do? Jump up and accuse Tony of lying, on top of everything else? He'll just deny it, anyway."

"Well, at least the judge will see Tony has friends to support him. They can throw the book at Tony, for all his father cares."

"His mother will defend him. I know that." My neck aches. I bend my head from side to side.

"Want a massage?" asks John, rubbing my neck before I have a chance to answer.

I let my shoulders relax. "That feels great." When my mother pulls up, I see she's wearing her straw hat with the red poppy. "This is serious," I tell her, sliding in front. "You only wear that hat for funerals and weddings."

"Let's hope this isn't a funeral," says John. He squeezes in front, next to me. "I bet you can't wait for Roxie and me to get our licenses, Mrs. Baskowitz. You must be tired of lugging kids around."

"I like it," says my mother. "But not now."

"No," he agrees. "This is a bad time." It's amazing how easily John understands her. I never worry that John's feeling uncomfortable around her. He just listens carefully and picks up on her expressions, the way I do.

The city built the juvenile court right next to the city jail. An ominous sign! A glass partition divides the two buildings, bordered by wide concrete walkways and narrow hedges. Mother swings into the parking lot and stops in a space near the entrance. "VISITORS" is painted on the blacktop in big white letters.

"Is there a place marked 'Offenders'?" John asks.

"What do we do now?" I say. "Are we supposed to walk right into the courtroom and sit down?"

Mother puts her hand on my knee. "Wait."

"Wait for what?"

"You will see." She has a mysterious look on her face.

"What do you know that we don't, Mrs. Baskowitz?" John leans across me to observe my mother.

She hunches her shoulders as if to say "I don't know." Climbing the steps to the court building is a boy and his parents. They walk with their heads lowered, as if they don't want anyone to notice them. Maybe half the punishment is the humiliation of being there at all. The boy thrusts his hands into his pockets. At first I think it's Tony, but it's not. Up the street I see the Sterns' long white car approaching slowly. Charles is at the wheel, his cap cocked to one side. John's noticed the car, too. I feel his body tense. Charles pulls into the parking lot several spaces away from us. Out of the back window stares a small face with round, blue eyes.

"There's Glo," I say. I see her but I can hardly believe it.

"You go to her, Roxie," says Mother. "We will stay here."

John pulls the door handle, and we both slide out. As I run toward the Sterns' Cadillac, the windows slide down and Glo, looking thin and forlorn, motions me inside. Next to her sits Maggie Stern. Her bright hair is pulled back into a neat bun, and she's wearing a navy-blue suit. "Are you all right?" I blurt, addressing the question to both of them at the same time.

"Get in, Roxie," says Maggie in a faltering voice. Her face looks pale, and there are dark circles under her eyes. Charles comes around and opens the front door for me. Then he pats my arm reassuringly, tips his hat, and ambles over to a stone bench near the hedge.

"Are you going into the courtroom?" I ask Glo. She turns her head away. I can tell she's fighting not to cry. "John and I wanted to give Tony some support." Still no response from Glo. I turn to Mrs. Stern. "Are you all right?" I ask again.

"Let's put it this way, I'm getting better," she says. "But it will take a long time. I came home just for a short visit." She reaches for Glo's hand.

"Glo," I say, "please talk to me. I've felt terrible these last few weeks." I realize how much I've missed her.

Glo raises her eyes to mine. "I've felt even worse. It seemed like everyone deserted me. First, Mother went away. Then you wouldn't come over. And I couldn't talk to Dad. I've felt so guilty about Tony I couldn't talk to him, either. But I was afraid to do anything about it," she says in a rush of words.

"Naturally, I was very upset when I received this note," Mrs. Stern says, pulling my crumpled RB stationery out of her purse. "I was so bogged down with my own problem, I hadn't even considered the girls. I decided to call your mother to find out if she knew what you were up to. All she would say was, 'Talk to Glo.'" I could hear my mother's slow, emphatic voice. "So I came home." She smiles at me. *"Right away."*

"When Mother suddenly appeared in my room," Glo says, "I knew I couldn't hold back any longer. I broke down and told her everything."

"And that's why we're here," concludes Mrs. Stern. "I don't want Glo to make the same mistakes I have over the years. I don't want her hiding from her problems and, worse, hurting someone else in the process. I told Ray this was one time he couldn't straighten things out—for either of us." We both look over at Glo, who's sitting unusually still.

"Does Tony know you're going to be here?" I ask.

"Not yet. I'm scared to death. This is . . ." She pauses, trying to find the right word. We look at each other.

". . . the pits," we say in the same breath. Then she smiles for the first time.

I look out the window at John, who's leaning against our car, trying to act calm. But he keeps glancing over at us. "John and I will go in with you," I say.

"No! You don't have to. I'm going to do this myself, without everyone hovering around trying to protect me. Whatever happens happens."

Charles knocks on the window. "It's four o'clock, Mrs. Stern. You all better go inside."

For a moment, Glo's mother seems to collapse into the seat. Then she sits up very straight. "It's going to be all right. We can handle this," she says slowly and deliberately, almost as if talking to herself.

"Good luck," I say.

"Will you call me later?" asks Glo. Her eyes are uncertain, hesitant, the old sureness gone. And now, instead of me wanting her approval, she wants mine, wants it desperately.

"Of course. It will all work out. I know it."

She nods. "I'm sorry, Roxie."

I have to look away because I'm going to cry. Glo, my Glo. What happened to my fun-loving friend? Who is this scared, diminished person? She doesn't look like a comet that would blaze across the sky. Maybe she never was. I think of that afternoon in Maggie's studio, the sun gleaming down through the skylight, casting her in a halo of light. I remember wanting to be like her—how I envied Glo. All my past images of the people I've loved or looked up to are like shadows behind me. I can't move back or re-create them. It's like our old house on Buckingham Drive. I remember everything about it, but I don't live there anymore. My heart has to let go. I watch Glo and Maggie walk toward the court building, two thin figures holding on to each other tightly. A few yards away, my mother takes off her hat, and then the door opens and John is standing there. He reaches for my hand to help me out. "After this, let's go home and finish that paint job."

F
Gre   Greenberg, Jan
           Exercises of the heart

DATE DUE

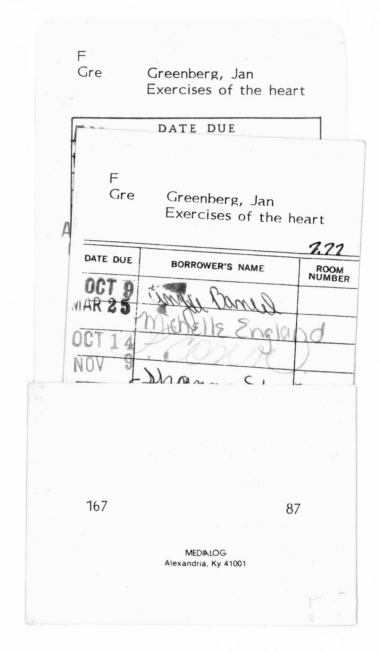

F
Gre   Greenberg, Jan
           Exercises of the heart

2.72

DATE DUE	BORROWER'S NAME	ROOM NUMBER
OCT 9	*Jingle Bonnie*	
MAR 25	Michelle England	
OCT 14		
NOV 9	*Thomas S*	

167   87